The Deep Blue Seize

Romesh Gopal, sitting in the private dining suite of the Ritz, wasn't listening to his diamond-dealing cousin from Amsterdam. He was staring at the antique blue and white Chinese porcelain dinner-plate in front of him and dreaming up his next scam.

All he would need was several thousand similar pieces and one eighteenth-century Dutch wreck sunk in two hundred feet of salt water and he would become a truly rich man.

But how to make everything watertight? Foolproof, that is.

Suddenly he saw it clearly. It was all a question of lateral thinking. Applied vertically.

Abandoning property development, he gathers together his fast-driving assistant Nigel Carlton, his nubile daughter Sharmila, and the rest of the deep-sea treasure-hunting team, and heads for the blue-green waters of the Outer Hebrides.

Moving at speed, the Gopal team and their converted trawler cross lines with salmon fishermen, solve the mystery of the sinister White Lodge, and triumph over some murderous rivals, until they present the 'find' at a truly explosive press conference.

All that remains thereafter is to get it (and themselves) back to the London auction rooms and they will become multi-millionaires . . .

DONALD McLARTY

THE DEEP BLUE SEIZE

COLLINS, 8 GRAFTON STREET, LONDON W1

William Collins Sons & Co. Ltd
London · Glasgow · Sydney · Auckland
Toronto · Johannesburg

For my father; and in memory of my mother,
who loved to read late into the night.

First published 1989
© Donald McLarty 1989

British Library Cataloguing in Publication Data

McLarty, Donald
    The deep blue seize.—(Crime Club)
    I. Title
    823'.914[F]

ISBN 0 00 232264 1

Photoset in Linotron Baskerville by
Rowland Phototypesetting Ltd
Bury St Edmunds, Suffolk
Printed in Great Britain by
William Collins Sons & Co. Ltd, Glasgow

CHAPTER 1

I growled at the dog. Bagha turned away without a word, then padded back across the gravel and round the bushes on the front lawn.

Irritable, I was even annoyed by the Gopal front door being open. I assumed it was to cool the rambling building.

I was not happy. My girlfriend was away, so I had had no Caroline for one whole week. And the journey from central London to the leafiest corner of Beckenham had taken five minutes more than usual. Without giving me the chance to cut anybody up. But the worst thing was the lack of direction. Being told by my employer that he didn't need me before mid-afternoon showed the state things had reached.

Inside the hall was the usual lingering smell of joss. Turning away from the faint noise of Heavy Metal coming from under the kitchen door, I passed the billiard room, and strolled down the corridor towards the usual door. The sign read 'Dad's Den'.

Romesh Gopal was using the tribal fly-whisk; more to circulate the air than to hit insects. He wasn't deep in the Business Section of his favourite newspaper, worrying about the state of his personal pension arrangements. Instead, he was reading a hardback.

In the warm air I peeled off my blazer and fitted it across the back of the outsized armchair. The one in zebra skin. As I rolled up the sleeves, my elbow almost snagged on the front fangs of the lion-head on the wall above the fireplace. I remembered just in time to shorten my arm swing.

At my light cough, Romesh looked up. He tossed the whisk on to the mock-Jacobean desk.

'Ah, you are timely. I need person to use as sounding-board.'

He used the ivory dagger which said 'Kampala' on the hilt to mark his place in the book.

With that sort of warning, I tried a diversion. 'So how was the freebie dinner with your cousin? Ritzy?'

I sat.

'Ritz was most enjoyable venue. It is always good to catch up with news of far-flung family enterprises in luxury setting.'

'Business in Holland still sparkling, then?'

'Amsterdam Gopals are making most of diamond trade, quite naturally. Otherwise there would be no private dining suite. No eating from antique dinner service. No presents for British branch of Gopals.'

He patted the lid of the new cigar box with the Dutch label, then picked up the glowing stub from the beaten-brass ashtray. It was the only hint of India in the room.

'Ashok was generous in every respect. Except in urge to share prosperity.' He shook his large head. 'We must go ahead on our own. Seeking fresh avenues of profit.'

He had got back to philosophy. His own, revenue-based, philosophy. I looked up to the ceiling to find the noise. For the first time that summer, the fan was whirring.

He picked up the book and waved the spine at me. The jerky movement was too fast for me to read.

'We must use Lateral Thinking technique from now on. We shall look everywhere for money-making ideas.' He slapped the cover.

'Mr de Bono is yet another person come to Britain to make good. He is from Malta, you understand. I was inspired to buy. Malta is almost Africa.'

I didn't feel up to hearing yet again about the Long March of the Gopal clan from Uganda to London, armed with British passports.

'Maybe *you* should write a book,' I said quickly.

'I am serious, Nigel! Property development market in UK is not buoyant. I can scarcely afford household upkeep.' His fat, hair-covered forearm waved through the humid air. 'If I am deprived of income, who would care for Sharmila at critical time in development?'

I didn't know whether he meant the shape of his only daughter or his latest profession. The conversation was getting out of hand again.

Suddenly I remembered his idea from the previous gloomy week. 'What happened to the Timeshare rip-off?'

He scowled. 'How can simple businessman defeat power of press? It is most unfair. Each day there are articles warning public of alleged pitfalls. I shall stop reading daily journals.' He threw the de Bono book on top of his copy of *The Times*.

Silence fell.

I sweated quietly into my only pink shirt in 100% cotton. It was into its second day, due to Caroline's trip.

The door opened behind me. The heels clicked until they reached the carpet.

'Heard your creepers on the doormat, Nige.' She put my mug down on the corner of the desk.

'Noisy in here, isn't it?' Sharmila said it into the silence. Then she bent over me, sticking out her chest. 'Like my sparklie? Dad brought it back. Present from my Dutch Uncle. Well, cousin.'

The tight mauve and silver material was already bright and tinselly. The diamond brooch was more discreet. It was pinned to the very top of the patterned band across her amazing bust.

'Thought you'd like to cast an eye.' Sharmila inhaled a second time, without straightening up. Caught in mid-sip of Darjeeling, I tried to re-focus.

'Nice.' I swallowed tea.

When I opened my eyes again, she was still twiddling her red fingernails behind the brooch to make it catch the sunlight.

'Real, they are. Well, the middle one is.'

She picked up the tray again and gave her father his tea, slipping an envelope under the saucer. 'Looks really borin', Dad.'

She stretched across to straighten the collar of his safari jacket, then swung back to me.

'Give you a preview of my sexy beach gear, if you like. Had to get somethin' for my hols, didn't I? Cost a bomb.'

She didn't wait for me to reply.

I stared at the photographs. She had moved on from last year's bikini to a one-piece. In the first three photographs the shoulder-straps were in three different positions. In the last shot, the top was held vaguely in place by her hands. I wondered who had taken them. Certainly not fond father.

I worked out what was odd about them. They had been taken on the Self-Timer in her frilly, half-in-focus bedroom. She must have balanced the camera on the dressing-table while she wiggled.

Remembering Romesh's attitude to his daughter, I kept my questions to the subject of where she would be going.

Suddenly he spluttered into his cigar. She tucked the photo wallet back into the taut waistband of the red stretch-pants.

'Must go. Got to brush up on the Portuguese for "Keep your hands off". See you, Nige!'

She turned on one high red heel, clipped the Walkman earphones back on, and left the room. The noise echoed down the long corridor.

'It is great concern,' said Romesh, putting down his teacup. I never knew what to say in reply to that.

He hadn't finished. 'And you should not excite young girls by staring at suggestive self-portraits.'

I didn't say anything back to him. I had long ago stopped arguing about imaginary attacks on his daughter's chastity.

He lay back and took a really deep breath.

'I have had major concept, Nigel.'

He blinked. 'I shall tell you as much as is necessary at this moment. I shall use "Need-to-Know" principle. In manner of British Secret Service.'

It was probably the humidity, I thought later, driving home. And the word 'concept' hadn't helped.

'Yes,' I told him. 'Don't let on too much about what's going to happen. Might affect my brain.'

His mouth stopped, half-open. He blinked again.

I barged on. 'Just tell me the simple bits. Leave in the fast-driving, of course, but don't load me up with any brain-work, whatever you do. I'm happy with you handling the really big concepts. Colonel Oliver North, that's me. Action Man.'

In the silence, I wondered whether I'd gone too far.

He had closed his mouth half way through my outburst.

'You are quite right, Nigel. I have been too careful of your welfare.' He blinked yet again. 'I must treat you in future as caring, thinking adult.'

I swallowed more tea.

'Yes,' he told me. 'To start, I shall brief you fully. Not "Need-to-Know". We shall share conceptual planning. Decision-making. Implementation.'

There was one abstract noun missing. 'And profit,' I said.

'And profit.' He seemed to say it more slowly.

He stretched sideways, to a bookshelf I hadn't seen before. With one item on it. He pulled the box file across to the desk, lifted the lid, and flipped up the clip. Then he peeled off the topmost newspaper cuttings. The Gopal filing system had been improved.

'As soon as I returned from Ritz, I followed up story.'

He tilted forward in his chair to wave the first clipping at me. It was from *The Times*. A large headline which said something ending in ... OF THE NANKING TREASURE.

I knew which word to zoom in on. 'Tell me about this treasure.'

He pointed to the photograph in the cutting. It showed an art auction being held in a swank hotel. A large Chinese plate was being held up.

He put his hands behind his head. 'Imagine huge amount of ancient porcelain, Nigel, found by gallant sea-captain in Dutch galleon at bottom of South China Sea. Story is most exciting.'

'Right.' Then I waited.

'He is suddenly millionaire! By selling off Chinese artefacts at highest prices in Amsterdam. They have great attraction. And why? Because of romance of deep-sea search!' He paused for breath. 'Even dull-dog such as Ashok was affected.'

Romesh saw that my brain had slid into neutral.

'Cousin Ashok. Diamond-dealing Gopal cousin. Who arranged that I should eat with him in private suite from antique Chinese tableware of eighteenth century, purchased and used by Ritz.'

'You ate off these fancy plates?' I was still goggling.

'We ate off such plates. Yes.' He said it patiently. 'Soup plates. Of deepest blue pattern. And white. Dinner plates also. And rice bowls, so delicate, from which to eat Ritz pudding.'

His expression was now very serious. 'And while Ashok chattered, I was using imagination.'

'You had this monumental concept over the Crêpes Suzette?'

'Exactly so.' He waggled his head sideways in the movement which always fooled me. Then he pushed his chair backwards with one chukka-booted foot, got up, and walked round the desk, hands in the pockets of his safari jacket. It spoiled the delicate curve of his stomach.

He stared down at me like an oversized Indian imp.

'Perhaps you can now guess such concept?' He strode past my chair.

I turned and spoke to the full head of black hair. 'We get some other skipper to find more submerged Chinese plates and flog them off to the punters direct.'

It stopped him in mid-stride. 'Almost so.'

I took a deep breath. 'Cousin Ashok does it all for us—and we give him a cut?'

Romesh spun round. 'Ashok will not be sharing! He is already too prosperous. And preoccupied with minerals.'

I was beginning to be sorry I'd got involved in concepts. 'Can't think,' I told him.

He went back to his chair and spoke quickly.

'Concept is most simple. *We* find wreck of sailing ship of eighteenth century. *We* profit from romance of sea!'

'But I don't see how all . . .'

He leaned across, twisted the next clipping around, and laid it on the near side of the desk, under my nose.

'Read statistic, kindly.'

I started to read them out. '100 full dinner services, 900 soup plates, 12,000 coffee cups . . .' I lifted my head.

'Read on, please. To real statistic.'

I could see no bigger numbers. I looked up a second time for help.

He stabbed at the piece of paper, his finger starting to pick up the printers' ink.

'Six times! That is most meaningful statistic.' He prodded again. 'Porcelain on ship became all at once six times value of same plates which can be purchased cheaply in London auction rooms. It was romance of galleon which made difference. Six times difference!'

I put down the mug. 'Romesh, what the hell do *we* actually know about sea-diving?' I had to take in more air. 'How could *we* find a treasure-boat full of ancient plates and yank them up from two hundred feet?'

'Up comes second, Nigel! First of all, we take plates down! That is lateral thinking! More certain. More controllable. Less risk.'

He patted the top of the de Bono book. 'Yes. Positively lateral. Unexpected downward movement to begin!'

'What are you talking about, Romesh?'

He leaned forward. 'Instead of seeking vessel full of uncertain treasure, we find empty wreck and fill with authentic Chinese porcelain. Then, with maximum publicity, we bring fragile pieces up from depths and make guaranteed large killing.'

He took a single, emotional breath. 'You must find me empty galleon.'

In the large garden I could see Bagha corner a bumble-bee. He was sitting, head to one side, deciding whether to swallow it.

Seeing that I had exhausted my mental capacity, Romesh looked down at the desk and saw the letter Sharmila had brought in earlier.

'Control of media will be paramount.' He opened the envelope. The letter was from the British Institute of Management. It had been the word 'British' that had made him join.

He waved the subscription request. 'It is vital to keep abreast of management aspects. Control. Supply. Demand.'

In the next ten minutes, I received my further orders.

'Which sale of ropey old china do we roll in on?' I asked, looking over the broad shoulder.

'Carruthers & Co. is next auction.' His finger had stopped running down the list of future art sales.

'That's Caroline's firm. Not on.'

'You told she is absent from workplace. I have assumed that was reason for Carlton irritability today, Nigel.'

I said nothing.

'She will be absent from post next Monday also?'

'Due back middle of next week.'

'Then it is in order to purchase antique tableware from firm. However, I can understand concern for lady, Nigel. It is most praiseworthy.'

He stood up to guide me out of the airless room.

In the corridor I shrugged on the blazer and straightened my tie in the mirror. The frame was ebony, carved in a swirling Hindu pattern—of gods about to have it off with bulging goddesses.

'I shall also use visit to auction rooms to observe techniques for future sale. After we have rescued from sea.'

'I'll tune up the car.' I coughed to get rid of his cigar smoke. 'We can use mine if our first bit of action is going to be honest.'

We had reached the front door.

'No fast getaways, Nigel. Early activity will most certainly be open and above board.' He giggled. 'You see! I am already using nautical jargon. It is something for you to practise also.'

He pushed me towards the MGB.

'I too shall not be idle. We must both acquire fresh expertise in new pastures.'

I corrected him. 'New waters.'

I stepped on to the gravel drive.

He had to call it out over the noise of the engine.

'Remember we are in need of suitably empty sunken vessel! I shall expect you to have begun research!' He waved a hand, twirled round on the doorstep, and disappeared into the house.

Bagha loped round the corner, tongue out in the July heat.

'How you got the name "Tiger", I shall never know,' I told him.

He barked at my rear wheels as they spat gravel into his teeth.

'Taken on as a driver,' I told the MGB dashboard. 'Re-deployed as a bloody diver.'

I pushed in the cassette. The jazz band fronted by Dicky Wells and Django Reinhardt, in Paris in 1937, was just hitting the first bars of its next number. It was 'Between the Devil and the Deep Blue Sea'.

CHAPTER 2

I twiddled my thumbs, stared at the unusual dashboard knobs and switches, and waited for him to come out of the house. It was 9.30 a.m., I was ahead of schedule. It gave me time to think back.

My driving was the reason I had landed the job with Romesh Gopal in the first place. The main reason anyway.

I had been in limbo-land; two painful years at a red-brick with nothing but re-sits to look forward to. No job prospect either, even with my school tie on. Just back from an amazing six-month stay with my Uncle Ray in good ole New Orleans, I had a super tan and a fistful of jazz cassettes. And not much else.

I was shacked up in what would have been called a squat if we hadn't been to good schools and shaved every second day.

The food parcel from my mother had been wrapped in the family newspaper. *The Times* had dropped from around the fruitcake and fallen open at the Sits. Vac. page. I had read as I munched.

The ad which leapt out had finished by saying: '. . . and must possess highest quality driving skills.'

The voice on the other end of the line had put me off until it promised my fare to Beckenham and back. That evening I had sent off my CV—he actually said 'Bio-data'— and my one good photograph.

Five non-working days had gone by, and then the summons came.

Finding Royal Avenue in greenest Beckenham without trouble, I had started to walk up the drive. The legs sticking out from under the smaller car were dressed in light khaki. It turned out to be a safari suit, suspiciously clean, I realized later. The car, in British racing green and about the size of a straw bale at Brand's Hatch, was a Mini.

He was Romesh Gopal, he told me, pushing that mane of hair back into place. He looked honest. He had asked if I tinkered as well as drove. I tinkered for him. The car had started first time. I didn't know it then, but I had passed my first real test.

Leading me down the enormous corridor into the 'den', he had sat me down and asked me to describe the occupier of the room we were in—going only from the décor and furnishings. He claimed it was to be my test as a potential man of property. He still looked honest.

I fluffed it. I had finished up, brilliantly I thought, by saying that the owner was obviously someone fresh off the Bombay boat. Sitting in the zebra armchair, I had been one continent out.

The rest of the hour was a monologue, not an interview. How he had suffered under the rule of Idi Amin in darkest Uganda, his place of birth. How, after losing his wife, he had struggled to transport himself and tiny daughter and British passport to Southall, Middlesex.

Romesh had then lit up another awful cigar and told me that he had lost money as a newsagent in Middlesex in the mid-1970s. He had looked very serious. He always is, about money.

To show him I was still awake, I asked a question.

'Because damned place was entirely infested with other Ugandan Asians being newsagents also!'

He had laughed. I had laughed too. To get the job.

As we chortled, I had peered at his desktop. My CV had been assaulted with Day-Glo pens. Looking at it upside down, I saw that my school, my photograph, and my driving skills had been highlighted in yellow. The gap I had left under Work Experience had been bashed in pink. Pink looked bad. Only later did I find out that it was his colour for extra Brownie points. I could make nothing of his notes in the margin—until it dawned on me they were in Bengali.

At that point, he had looked at his watch, got up, and led me to the door. I coughed and tightened the knot in my tie. He smiled yet again. We walked, out to the Mini. Still nothing. I coughed again and scuffled pebbles with one suede toe. But no sign of a progress report on how I had got on.

'You will drive, kindly. Top speed. To railway station where Sharmila is arriving.' He had turned into the complete, caring parent.

I didn't know it then either, but my second real test had begun.

As the tiny wheels scarred the gravel, I realized that someone had souped up the engine. Romesh's knuckles had whitened at my driving. He had had to start his sentence again.

'Sorry, Mr Gopal?'

'I said I shall tell more tomorrow, Mr Carlton. When you

have first proper day of employment.' I had really tramped on the pedal then.

Five fast minutes later, screeching to a stop outside Beckenham station, I had met the delicious, forbidden Sharmila.

All that had been three years ago, of course, and her body was then attacking a taut black school uniform. It was clear why he was being protective. It was to be the start of my other problem with women.

But everything that bright spring day had seemed straightforward, above board. Honest.

I reminded myself that it was how he had described the first part of the action in his latest scam as I heard his heavy feet on the gravel on the morning of the Carruthers auction. He flopped into the passenger seat. I started up and stepped on the accelerator. 'Nought to sixty in twenty minutes. Wow.'

That was when he said, 'Drive carefully, please. Remember we are now much wider than Carlton MGB.'

'So would you be, Bwana. If you'd been stuffed full of straw and old blankets.'

I tugged my cloth cap to a less servile angle and tried to hide my disgust at driving a rented van towards an elite set of Bond Street auction rooms.

He was unmoved. 'We are about to buy great amount of fragile porcelain, Nigel. Large transport vehicle is therefore necessary. I trust you will drive more slowly on return journey.' My MGB had finally been put aside.

Silence fell, except for the rattle from the engine. Its note annoyed and frustrated me. And I hate Monday mornings.

By the time we got to Southwark, I was getting used to the size of the van. I steamed round à double-decker and suddenly felt relaxed enough to pass on good news.

'Made quite a lot of progress. Signed on at the sub-aqua—'

'I am not sure we have sufficient straw. Perhaps we should have also accepted pillows Sharmila offered.'

'When I'm well on the way to winning my water-wings, I'm going to really get down to searching for that—'

'Perhaps it would be more appropriate after saleroom success if I am one to stack up tableware. I shall stand in rear of vehicle while you pass each stack of plates carefully to me.'

I gave up.

The streets after Waterloo Bridge had their usual mid-morning snarl-ups. The Trafalgar Square traffic was relatively civilized, until the rain started.

After two more minutes I had to switch the wipers to their faster speed. Then I trod on the brakes to miss an old lady, bent under an umbrella. Romesh used his stiffened arm to keep his back against the seat.

'When auction commences, please leave bidding solely to me. It is my name on registration form. I who have bidder's reference number.' He waved a gold-edged card bearing three large digits under my nose.

'I'll sit on my hands. Just in case I sneeze and you land up with something expensive from the Ming Dynasty.'

'I have inspected porcelain at formal viewing last week. And fixed in mind maximum prices we can afford to offer auctioneer. But I must have no distraction at bidding.'

I put it down to nerves. 'Try not to worry about it,' I told him, and wrenched the wheel to swing into Lower Regent Street.'

'Exactly so,' he replied, but without the head-waggle. He was too intent on grabbing the strap to stay upright.

We drove on

Looking quickly across, I saw that he had started to do

sums on the inside front page of a glossy art catalogue. They were all multiplications. By a power of six. With pound signs.

'You reckon we can actually get all these piles of plates at a decent price?' I asked after a hundred more yards.

'Bidding limits will be nicely judged. I have already said.' He lay back against the black plastic seat.

Remembering an old Caroline hint about Bond Street parking, I balanced the near-side wheels on the sliver of pavement in the tiny cul-de-sac and pulled on the hand-brake.

'Smart-ass!' I said it suddenly. Immediately behind us, another driver was using the same kerb-drill, but only to deposit his passenger.

Just as Romesh, in his only dark business suit, stepped on to the pavement, he was nudged off-balance by someone in a long white robe, someone else in a hurry. Romesh had to use the tip of his rolled umbrella to avoid a foot in a lake-sized puddle.

'Damned Mohammedan! They are worse than tourists! Why should we British suffer for high temperatures in Persian Gulf?'

'His man in the peaked cap handles a nifty stretched limo, though.' I had been admiring the turning skills of the chauffeur in the maroon uniform.

'I can only hope surgical operation in Harley Street will go badly for his employer.' Romesh was still staring curved daggers at the disappearing white robe.

'Not today it won't. Looks like you've got a fellow-traveller.' The Arab was also making for the Carruthers front doors.

We passed the two art-book shops and the jewellers. The entrance to the auction rooms was as grand as ever. Keeping my cap brim low to avoid being recognized by colleagues of Caroline who might remember me from a party, I strode up the marble stairs past the security guard and held the polished doors open for my employer.

We walked up the long, carpeted stairs to the main auction room. I flicked through the first pages of Romesh's sale catalogue.

'You allowed for Buyer's Premium and VAT when you were making those calcs?'

I didn't get a reply.

'Wouldn't worry about it. They whack the sellers too, if I read this correctly. They call it commission, actually. Sounds down-market to me. Ten per cent unless the stuff gets a poor price, then they promise to hit you for twelve and a half. Plus you-know-what. Unless you're an Arab or something. It says here that foreign residents flogging off the family silver don't have to pay VAT. Think our Sheik up front is a buyer or a seller?'

I knew the effect it would all have. Romesh stalked across the landing clutching his gold-edged card, pretending not to have heard.

The room was high-ceilinged, with an amazing mixture of art around the walls. No attempt had been made to sort it out, or even to line it up. In front of a gloomy German landscape and a Venetian canal scene, most of the pricier items in that day's sale perched at different heights on a row of third-rate French and English furniture.

Romesh chose the best fake Chippendale armchair in the second row of seats and patted the arm of the next chair. I sat down beside him. It creaked.

We had arrived ten minutes ahead of the genteel 11.0 a.m. schedule. Romesh started to watch the other arrivals.

I searched the catalogue. 'No pics of the stuff we're after that I can see. Is that good or bad?'

He took the book from me. 'Prices for such lots will be

more reasonable. I shall offer auctioneer's highest esti-
mation.'

He turned to a back page, and began to underline the
printed amounts.

I looked round. People were beginning to turn away from
the displays and take their seats in the rows in front of or
to the side of the wooden lectern. Some leaned against the
back wall. Two youngish Chinese with trendy hair and
track shoes were admiring a huge, multi-coloured dish. A
pair of dapper Japanese bankers on a day off hovered
by the double doors. The American dealers behind them
stopped talking dollars. There were at least fifty people in
the room.

Sharply at eleven, the Carruthers staff standing behind
the makeshift barrier of antique tables parted and a skinny
man in a freakish tie and black pinstripe suit stepped up to
the high desk. He picked up the gavel but didn't use it.
Instead, he cut into the buzz of talk with a high, dry cough.

'Good morning, Ladies and Gentlemen. Welcome to
another prestigious sale of fine Chinese Export porcelain by
Carruthers & Co.' The voice was deeper than I expected.

'Without more ado, then, let us turn to Lot No. 1. Two
of these, showing one, a fine pair of *famille rose* pink-ground
baluster vases. Late Qing dynasty.' He breathed for the first
time.

'A lot of interest in these. Shall I say one thousand five
hundred?'

Romesh shifted in his chair.

From the pitched ceiling, above the blank chandelier, I
could still hear the rain. Gradually, my attention began to
flag. I started to think of Caroline and her new tan.

I forced myself back to the sale. The auctioneer was using
the fancy words I had seen in the catalogue. 'Quatrefoil',
'Baluster', 'Oviform', 'Cloisonné'.

After two minutes I decided to stop trying to guess at

what they meant. I yawned and looked left. Like everyone else in the room, Romesh was solemnly writing down the amounts of the successful bids against the catalogue entries. He looked up and saw my expression.

'Remember,' he whispered, 'when we return triumphantly from sea, it will be our items in vanguard of next auction.'

I grunted.

More time passed. The lots moved through the expensive dynasties to names I had never heard of. The auctioneer had left the five- and four-figure bid amounts behind. He was beginning to sound bored too. He had stopped using words like 'vibrant' and started to call some pieces 'amusing'.

'How much longer before we get to the remainders?' I asked out of the corner of my mouth.

He frowned and flipped a single glossy page to get to where his bidder's card lay, acting as a bookmark.

'Right,' I replied.

I looked round as several of the audience began to leave. Two of the staff from behind the tables slid out by a side door.

'Lot No. 172.'

Romesh sat up.

'A small set of twenty-four plates, blue and white, circa 1750. Shall we start at four hundred pounds?'

Romesh wiggled forward in his seat. I peered across and down to his open glossy page. The higher estimate had been boldly underlined. It read £700.

I had forgotten about him, but as soon as the auctioneer looked up from his list, Romesh's new-found friend, the Arab, waved his hand from the second side-row.

'Thank you, sir.' The auctioneer gave an elaborate bow.

Two more bidders came in, then fell away. Romesh was now sitting bolt upright.

As soon as the auctioneer got to £700, Romesh's hand twitched.

'Is that a bid, sir?'

'Yes, kindly.'

'Thank you, sir.' No bow.

'And eighty?'

The Arab waved. Romesh snorted.

Nobody said anything to the auctioneer's next question. 'Still with the original bidder at seven hundred and sixty,' he added, and paused.

'Have you a number, sir?'

The Arab waved his gold-edged card.

'No. 435. Thank you, sir.'

'Damned vogs!' hissed Romesh. 'Stripping country bare.' He put a large cross through the printed £700 he had underlined earlier.

The result of the next bidding round was exactly the same. Romesh entered, then found he had exited, at the top estimate price. The Arab, now the lone bidder, won his prize at the very next step up the auctioneer's scale of bid amounts.

As the next fifteen lots went through, the size of each set of porcelain got bigger. They were now being pointed out by the auctioneer waving his gavel at a full trolley, pushed along by a porter in a green apron.

By the third winning bid, the auctioneer had stopped asking for an Arab reference number.

'Now they are on damned nod and vink basis,' muttered Romesh. 'How do ve know they are not in cahoots?'

It was the second time he had mangled his w's. He was upset.

I nodded back. By my own count, we had now missed out on over a thousand antique Chinese plates and rice bowls. I started to imagine an empty drive home. It was time for sympathy.

'Probably for his wives, Romesh. Coffee mornings in the Gulf tend to get crowded, I reck—'

All at once, I stopped consoling. Living proof of my idea had turned up.

The shrouded figure in dark brown had almost reached her husband. She put down the green Harrods carrier and stacked the Asprey parcel against it. It gave off an expensive clinking noise. The veiled lady began to whisper news of her shopping expedition into a white-covered ear. I saw that the fine black stockings peeping from below the plain cotton had tiny lace ankle-bows.

It came as a sharp hiss.

'Nigel! You will move quickly. Obtain Arabian reference ticket.'

He gave a brisk nod towards the side-row.

'While attention is elsewhere!'

I opened my mouth. Romesh pushed me.

'What's the point getting me to nick this?' I demanded, slipping the card into the waiting hand. 'The Sheik and the bod playing with the gavel both know the rotten number by heart.'

He put the card into his inside pocket and said nothing. I sat down.

For the last time, the auctioneer sighed. 'Final lot for today, Ladies and Gentlemen. Again for the Dutch market, a set of one hundred and forty-four pieces. Quite nice. Shall we start at . . .'

Again Romesh lost, by one bid-step. The tired auctioneer wrote down No. 435 without looking up.

'I don't get it.' I was tripping down the stairs after him. We were both close behind the Arab couple. Progress was slow due to two sets of flowing robes being hoisted. Romesh didn't reply. We rounded the corner under the sign which said 'Settlements'.

'Try not to worry about it. Next time I'll get a pointer or two from Caroline first. How to handle the cheapo end of the porcelain market. Now, if I can get it back quick enough, we'll save a day's rental on the—'

He was tearing up his own gold-edged reference number. 'Romesh, aren't you supposed to hand—'

He had also been watching the Arab unroll a huge wad of notes at the first till. Using a painful elbow grip, he spun me round to face the front doors.

'Nigel! You will now drive us most quickly, please. To rear of auction rooms.'

He was rummaging inside his business suit.

CHAPTER 3

It had stopped raining. We had to narrow our eyes in the hard sunlight as we ran back to the cul-de-sac.

At the van, Romesh gave me back the reference number card stolen from the Arab. 'I must appear empty-handed.'

Struggling to find the lock, I shoved the gold-edged card into a pocket and wrenched the door sideways.

'Good God!' The hot air trapped inside the van hit me in the face. Romesh rapidly belted himself into the passenger seat. 'Backwards, kindly! We are fortunately in correct location.' He had already grabbed the diagonal strap and turned round to see where we'd be going.

I meshed the gears and tramped on the accelerator. The van careered backwards. Two fast turns of the wheel and we were round the tight right-angle in the alleyway. Through the rear windows, I could see the high red doors.

I twisted round, pushing my head out of the still-open van door.

'That's really ace. We've found the local fire-station.' Then I recognized the auctioneers' name again.

Romesh was already unbuckled. He jumped down ahead of me, scooped up a handful of mud, and plastered it across the van's rear number-plate. Before my feet touched the short ramp leading to the Carruthers store-room, he had rushed through the smaller red side-door.

I stuck my head through the doorway to see him bearing down on a man in a pair of brown overalls. He also wore the brown jacket of an overseer. His back was turned and, armed with a long inventory, he was examining porcelain, piled high on a trolley. Romesh turned and silently pointed out to me the flight of wooden stairs leading up to the Carruthers auction rooms. Then he held up one finger, stepped forward, and tapped the foreman lightly on the shoulder with his rolled umbrella.

'This is collection point, please? My goods are ready for transportation?' He reached across and picked up the top plate from one of the piles.

'You the Arab gentleman, sir?' He had obviously never seen a customer quite like Romesh. His wide eyes started at the highly polished shoes. He took the plate from Romesh's hand and finished his inspection by staring at the umbrella. He hadn't enjoyed being touched.

'Can't give you a sniff of the merchandise without a sight of your reference, sir.' There was a distinct pause between the last two words.

Romesh continued to stick out his chest.

'My driver will provide,' he told him. He patted his side pockets to show how short of money he was and, with a tight bow, turned back towards me. I was standing just inside the doors.

'George. Kindly.'

I tugged at the cap brim and came forward, hands travelling around my own pockets. After a rapid search, I found the gold-edged card and thrust it at the man who pays my wages.

'Sorry, Your Excellency. Forgot you'd passed it across.'

My sudden South-East London whine caused him to blink, but he took the card and gave it to the foreman without a downward glance.

'That'll do nicely, sir,' said the man.

Romesh remained straight-faced. 'Please release goods as quickly as possible,' he said. 'We are on double yellow line.'

The foreman very slowly checked the number against the entries on his listing. After two minutes, he nodded to two assistants who had just finished pushing two more porcelain-laden trolleys from the goods lift in the far corner. They were enjoying the side-show.

One of the assistants began to open the other high door while his companion started to marshall the trolleys.

'Edge up a bit wiv the transport, Georgie,' the older of the two men told me. 'Then we can see about earning that gi-normous tip from His Esteemed Highness or whatever.' He winked without smiling. 'You know, the old baksheesh caper.'

The younger one had a question too. He asked it as I clambered back into the van. 'Don't he do anything for himself? You get to open up the old brolley too, I suppose?'

I ignored them, backed through the gap in the high red doors and opened up the van from the inside. The doors were very stiff.

They started to pass the plates and bowls so quickly I had barely enough time to kick the blankets and straw into position. As I sweated, I could see from under my cap brim that Romesh's rolled umbrella was tapping out a tattoo on the store-room floor. Sucking in air, I lifted my head to ask for help and saw what he was really doing. As the assistants went past him with armfuls of porcelain, Romesh was watching the top of the wooden stairs.

Just as the final stacks of plates were loaded on the floor of the van, the foreman left his desk at the rear of the dark room. He'd been thinking.

'How do I know you've actually paid, Your Excellency?' He smirked.

To answer him, Romesh had to turn round.

'Paperwork is quite in order. My bearer will come down from . . .'

He was about to turn back, hand outstretched in a wide Arab gesture to point out the door at the top of the wooden stairs, when I heard the faint click of the knob. I was bent double, taking the full weight of the last load. I looked up quickly. My field of vision cut in half by the brim, I could just make out the bottom twelve inches of white robe and the brown Oxford shoe hitting the highest wooden step.

'Romesh!' I nodded abruptly past his shoulder, dropped the plates on the naked metal floor of the van, and slammed shut the rear doors in the face of the other assistant.

Romesh knew without looking round.

The foreman, still unsuspecting, had turned towards the stairs. He called up to the real purchaser, 'Come on, Abdul! Let's have that bit of yellow paper, then. Your boss is keen to get mobile!' He held out his hand for the receipt.

The Arab's face did not believe it.

'Very quickly, kindly!'

Romesh's bottom hit the warm plastic of the seat next to me just as I meshed the gears and pointed the van's front wheels through the wide doorway and down the ramp.

I charged the big van past the stretched limousine; past the amazed chauffeur in his maroon peaked cap. One fast twist of the steering-wheel and we were back in Bond Street. Two hundred yards and another twirl and we had left the art world behind.

'Slow, kindly! I need not tell you we have fragile, costly cargo on board.'

I resented that.

Safely across the Thames once more, I looked up through the upper left corner of the windscreen searching for the sign for the Elephant and Castle. I saw it at last, hidden by a rain-soaked tree, and felt more relaxed.

'This sub-aqua club I joined Friday, friendly lot. Take you through in easy stages. Theory first—all about oxygen, nitrogen narcosis and suchlike. I'll need more money, though. Rental of cylinders and the other heavy gear. Thought I looked pretty sharp in flippers and mask, between you and me.'

But as I had started to speak, Romesh's worries about the porcelain took over. He wriggled out of his seat and clambered into the back of the van. In the mirror, I could see him fuss with a pile of swaying soup bowls, then wedge himself into a corner by the doors, brace his feet gingerly against two of the highest stacks, and steady two others with his hands. The rattling noises died away.

At the Elephant at last, I steered carefully round the giant roundabout and threaded the van through the growing traffic towards the correct exit.

'Next session I get to submerge completely in ten feet of chlorinated water. We train in teams of two. Not sure about the Kiss of Life bit, I must say. No women in our squad.'

We drove on. Suddenly a thought occurred to me. He was usually able to do two things at once. Such as holding down and hearing.

'Romesh, have you been listening to anything I . . .'

I looked in the mirror a second time. He was doing two things. He was scribbling figures on the back cover of the

Carruthers catalogue. He looked towards the front with a smug expression.

'I have completed costings, Nigel. We have obtained four thousand items. At hypothetical purchase price of one hundred and fifty thousand pounds.' He stopped to put in a comma.

'We multiply by six times, as I have said. Profit will be nine hundred thousand pounds, Nigel! Less rental of survey equipment and so on, less cost of raw materials.' He patted one stack of plates.

'Except that we have not paid material cost.'

Even out of the darkness of the back of the van, I could see his teeth gleam.

'I have almost forgotten. I have not allowed for avoided Buyer's Premium! Or Value Added Taxation.'

I could hear him finding a more comfortable spot for his rear. The cheerful humming of a man who had not previously dealt in positive taxation reached my ears.

'That is most satisfactory,' he said. 'White-collar, non-violent crime, Nigel, is to be preferred.'

I said nothing. It had all seemed so different on my second day at Romesh Gopal, Inc.

He had started by dodging around the subject of Pay As You Earn and Graduated National Insurance—they had seemed to upset him. Instead he told me about his first career switch in the UK—out of newspapers, lost Sunday supplements, Sellotape and glue and into the world of property development. How an austere developer could avoid taxation; how cash-in-hand was the thing. His eyes had shone. And how brilliant property deals had given him all this. He had waved the stub of yet another cigar around the room and at the huge garden behind him. I had crossed my newly-creased trouser-legs again.

He was still looking honest, sort of.

'But that was in years of boom, Nigel,' he had added,

and planted the chukka boots on the edge of the pulled-out drawer. 'Now second change of direction, in middle of 'eighties, is called for. And you will be part of!'

Now, three years and four close shaves further on, even our current ploy seemed to have turned into something physical.

But who was I to argue? I was in it mainly for the fast driving. I drove on.

We zipped along Beckenham High Street in silence and were soon crunching the Gopal gravel.

Bagha sniffed the first heap of plates which Romesh had taken from me and laid on the drive. Then he lost interest and loped back to his favourite corner of the back garden.

Romesh disappeared into the house. A minute later, the heavy doors to the garage slowly slid apart. I lined up the van alongside my MGB.

It was now even hotter. I pulled off the damp cap and threw it forward into the driver's seat.

'Couldn't Sharmila give us a hand with these?' I wailed as I slid a really awkward stack of china across the floor of the van and towards the open metal doors.

He turned from his own pile of porcelain against the garage wall and mopped his brow. His braces were bright red. 'We must not involve as yet. "Need to Know" basis.'

I pressed on, just as over-heated, passing each teetering stack to my sweating employer.

On one leg, I picked straw from my sock. Losing my balance, my free foot crashed on to the concrete floor, missing some ancient saucers by inches.

'Take more care, Nigel! Do you not realize single porcelain plate is now worth hypothetical one hundred and eighty pounds?'

It made me swear under my breath.

'What is difficulty?'

'Just wondering what the next move in the Snakes and Ladders will be,' I lied.

He straightened up, rubbing the small of his back with one fat knuckle. Then he limped painfully across to lock the garage doors and pick up the jacket of his suit. He turned round again.

'Before we decide, I have still to hear of progress you have made in finding suitably empty sunken vessel. You have not told.'

I began to splutter.

'Or even about success in gaining undersea skills, Nigel.'

CHAPTER 4

'Everybody up!'

I slammed the armful of books on to the top of his desk.

Romesh twitched and opened his eyes. 'I was not asleep! Contemplation is best with eyes closed.' He took his feet off the edge of the drawer and planted them on the carpet.

I sat down in the zebra-skin armchair.

He was still on the defensive. 'I have been considering future sale of porcelain. We must hold auction in most luxurious surroundings. Hilton, maybe. Even Ritz. To encourage highest bidding.'

'Shouldn't we get the stuff into the water first?' I asked, but he was too busy trying to read book titles.

I squared up the pile, then swung them round so that their spines faced him. I patted the top volume. 'Thought I could save you money. Went to the local library.'

He didn't look particularly impressed. 'You have found sunken vessel?' he asked me instead.

'Found lots of boats. An endless supply of beautiful wrecks

for you.' I dropped the pile. The noise made him jump. And go defensive again.

He pulled open another drawer. 'I too have been hard at work on basic data,' he claimed. He had resurrected his old clipboard. It bulged with newspaper cuttings. 'I have been re-reading. We can learn great deal from journalists.'

'What about today's headline?' I asked him.

He frowned.

'You know: FAMOUS AUCTION HOUSE SUFFERS DRAMATIC LOSS. "I WAS ROBBED," CLAIMS DESERT CHIEFTAIN.'

He took a deep breath. 'You do not understand commercial mind, Nigel. Who would then take property to auction people in future if Carruthers tell pressmen? They will be discreet. It is endearing characteristic.' He changed the subject. 'I have also been preparing original paperwork.' This time he pulled a double sheet of paper from his middle drawer. 'We must proceed in systematic way. We have left world of art behind. I have composed Critical Path.'

Ever since he had taken a computer course last year, he had been keen on what he called Critical Path diagrams. As far as I was concerned, the fancy name simply meant a long list of things to be done in a certain order. Mostly by me. I called it the 'work sheet'.

I always ignored his fancy coloured-pencil marks, with times and dates, which he scratched in on the right-hand side of each big sheet. What mattered was what he had written down on the left.

I craned forward to read. 'Why have you put "Obtain equipment" in red? We rent instead of buy? Is that it?'

'Because it is task for you,' he told me. 'I am now using colour-coding to show who will take relevant action.'

I kept looking. 'I'm down for quite a few, then.'

I read on. '"Obtain reference books". Done that. "Join

sub-aqua club". That's going swimmingly.' I scanned the whole list. 'You haven't got a line about the wreck.'

'It is in blue. Romesh Gopal colour. You will notice appropriate sentence. It begins with action-verb, "Analyse . . ."'

I sat back in the chair. 'Good word. What does it actually mean?'

'While you are completing undersea training and re-searching into equipment needs, I shall study books as well as cuttings from press. I shall then select best potential wrecked vessel. Allowing for maximum risk reduction.'

'You mean cutting down the chances of being spotted putting the porcelain down into its watery grave?'

'If you wish.' He looked prim.

I leaned forward. 'We can pick our wreck now. No need for prolonged intellectual study.'

I reckoned he was over-emphasizing the brainwork. Gopal brainwork. Besides, it was raining again.

I patted the top book. It was *A Night to Remember*, by Walter Lord.

'How about the *Titanic*? Had a quick flip through on the train.'

He wasn't pleased. '*Titanic* is highly unsuitable! Already journalists are there.'

'Thought you liked the press? Or cuttings, at any rate.'

He ignored that.

'French salvage persons too. Also it is in deepest sea. Off America. Highly unsuitable. You are being deliberately obtuse.'

I picked up the next book. 'OK, if you don't like that one, I've got the *Medina* for you.

'Tell.'

I flipped it open at the title page. On the opposite sheet was a photograph of a warship with full steam up, flying the Union Jack. I thought he would like that.

THE DEEP BLUE SEIZE

'Off Start Point. Devon. Full of antique Indian stuff. Sunk by a Kraut submarine at the end of World War One. We could make out there was also Chinese porcelain on board. Pillaged by grasping colonials coming home to retire.'

He winced. 'It is too late.'

'They haven't got it all up yet. We could sneak along one dark night.'

'I am meaning *boat* is too late, Nigel. It is not believable that vessel of early twentieth century sailing from India has cargo of Chinese porcelain from eighteenth.'

'Just thought it would save me some swimming. It's only six miles out.'

'That is single point in favour. But you have reminded me.'

He suddenly picked up the telephone and hit buttons.

'What's the problem?' I asked, but I was too late.

'Gregory Taylor, kindly.'

He was asking to be put through to his lawyer. His shady lawyer.

He twiddled his fingers as he waited.

'Gregory! It is Gopal. I am about to write novel.'

I heard a metallic crackle of surprise.

'I am serious! It will be exciting work of fiction.'

More questioning crackle.

'No. It is pastime only.'

He changed hands.

'But you must assist with one technical point, Gregory. Regarding position of imaginary sunken vessel. So that supposed cargo may be outside jurisdiction of UK.'

I could hear the static tell my boss the usual legal thing. That law man would have to speak to other law man.

'I shall await return call.'

Romesh put down the hand-set.

We talked about this and that. He worked his fingers some more.

The phone jangled. He picked it up and listened.

'You are saying that fellow partner considers that boat and cargo should be hypothetically placed more than twelve miles off UK coast?'

I heard more crackle and pop.

'Kindly do *not* seek out more informed maritime law opinion! Do not ask question of QC!'

Romesh had just paid his latest legal bill.

He put the telephone down.

'He's a shyster, Romesh. His legal mates are shysters too. How do you know we can actually rely on the word of a couple of—?'

He was scowling at me.

'Gopal legal opinion is that reasonable doubt exists regarding application of UK sea laws to international waters. We need such waters, Nigel. So as not to be deprived of hard-won capital gain.'

'See what you mean. Have to swim out a bit further, then. Goodbye *Medina*.'

I added the book to the reject pile. He was already craning to read the next title.

'How do you feel about Tobermory?' I asked. It was *The Tobermory Treasure* by Alison McLeay.

'It is Ireland?' he asked hopefully. 'Perhaps there are different laws.'

'Haven't dipped into it yet.'

There was a sudden noise behind me.

Her high heels clicked across the floorboards before she reached the carpet. 'Thought you two would be a bit peckish. All that brainwork.' Sharmila laid the tray down and dealt out the coffees.

There was a silence. I looked from one Gopal to the other and decided to help her.

'How're the holiday preps going? Escudos all lined up?'

She was still looking at her father. 'Still kittin' out, aren't I, Nige? Got to impress the local talent that London girls . . .'

'Sharmila,' he asked sharply, 'what is bowl?'

'Bombay Mix, Dad. The one you like.'

'Not what is *in* bowl, Daughter. I am asking about bowl itself.'

'Got it from the garage. Thought you could spare one.' She had filled the delicate porcelain soup bowl with some snacky bits.

Her father snatched it from her and abruptly dumped the contents into the empty elephant's foot he used as a paper bin.

'You will return at once.' He handed it back to her with a rigid arm. 'At once.'

'Not another of your capers, is it, Dad?'

'Why do you ask such question?'

'*I* saw you and Nige sneak in yesterday. Thought I wouldn't notice, I expect. I was at the washin' up, wasn't I? Someone's got to do it.'

'They were acquired legitimately. Purchased at auction sale in West End.'

'Dad.'

'Each item has . . .'

'Why were the two of you peerin' over your shoulders, then?'

'Kindly return porcelain straightaway to garage.'

'I'll just wash it out.'

'Straightaway, young lady.'

Sharmila stalked towards the door. 'Really lookin' forward to my first holiday on my own,' she told me as she passed.

The door slammed. Soon there was the sound of a heavier door being banged shut. Followed by pop music.

*

'It is great concern,' said Romesh.

'Tobermory is in Bonnie Scotland,' I said firmly, then looked at my digital watch.

'Wreck is far from coast?'

'Don't know yet. They've got a lot of salt water up there. Mull is past Rhum, Eigg, and Muck, going right, I think. Upper left on the map.'

I swallowed two tiny shreds of the snacky stuff which had fallen on the corner of the desk. They were burning hot. I began to splutter.

'It must be minimum twelve miles from shore, Nigel.'

'I'll have to read it up. Analyse it.' My mouth still on fire, I put the book under my arm and stood up. 'Must be off. Promised to provide Caroline with one full animal to come home to tonight.'

I pushed the last book at him. 'That leaves you with the real heavy.' It was *Shipwrecks of Great Britain and Ireland* by Richard Larn.

It had the opposite effect to the one I meant.

'Exactly so.' He waggled his head. 'Wreck must be in British Isles. To reduce transportation costs. This is to be business proposition, not joy-ride. And we must have land-base where trust is paramount.'

I gave him a sideways look. 'We certainly don't want any other villains flitting around our wreck. That wouldn't be on.'

The irony was lost on him. 'Exactly so. I am already attracted to idea of Scotland. Tobermory. Scottish people are most cost-conscious.'

I didn't argue.

He smoothed out his double sheet of paper. 'I shall continue to perfect Critical Path. Timing will be vital. I shall also make list of criteria for target vessel. It is important that risk element is at minimum.'

He had said that before, I told myself as I started to walk towards the door, the Tobermory book under my arm. I was already looking forward to driving the MGB again, having left it overnight in the Gopal garage while I returned the rented van.

He was now bending over his giant work sheet, writing between two lines and talking to himself. The bit I caught sounded like, '. . . British Maritime Protection Act 1973. Obtain copy.'

Fortunately he was writing it in blue.

'Got to go, Romesh. See a man about a cat.'

CHAPTER 5

I had parked the MGB outside her flat. I tossed the tin of cat-food from one hand to the other, then tucked the book on the Tobermory Treasure under one arm. It would pass the time until she turned up.

I was still carrying out a labour of love for my other female problem. The one I had met up with at the first bottle party after I had joined the Gopal clan. The fair hair was no difficulty. Or separate flats. Or even that Caroline could be hard to handle. It was mainly that she thought in straight and truthful lines—even though she did work in the art world.

It meant that I had to make out all the time that I was engaged in honest work and paid my taxes. And she thought, only seeing him in short spurts, that Romesh was cuddly. Cuddly but offering no great prospects of advancement. There was another difficulty—my other problem. Sharmila. Caroline did not understand why I had to deal with the girl. Giving me full credit for no strength of character, she was convinced I was being constantly lured towards a teenaged bedroom by what she called my personal child-bride.

That was one of the more polite ways she put it. I had pleaded reason. Why let myself be chased by the boss's daughter when I had a perfectly good, dazzling blonde? I even meant it. It didn't always work.

Anyway, head down into the light summer rain, I skipped up the short flight of sandstone steps, juggling with the key-ring. I was brought to a rapid halt by the large, powder-blue suitcase blocking my way. It was good news, but too-soon good news.

Book and tin slithering under one elbow, I was just able to struggle up the longer inside stairs to her door. Unlocking the door, I stepped into the tiny hall. There was only one, slight, sound. It was a cat purring. Feet still in the hall, I poked my head round the kitchen door.

She said it without even looking up. 'Rupert, this is Carlton. Carlton, Rupert. I don't believe you two have met.'

I dropped the heavy case in the hall and stepped forward. 'Do you realize that little rat has gone through your entire stock? Six tins of the stuff? He's having you on, woman.'

'Rupert is a cat, not a rat.'

I crashed his fresh tin on to the work-surface. 'Tin number seven. Representing two whole meals. Or it was until you gave him the whole of that one.'

'Good thing I dropped off at Tesco on the way back, that's all I can say, Carlton.' She folded her arms. Their colour was shown off by the flimsy white top and skirt she wore. The two-inch gap above the blue and red waistband of the white skirt was also bronzed.

'He's a complete bloody fraud.' I stared down at the cat.

Rupert felt hostile eyes on him and looked up in mid-gulp. Then he lowered his head and attacked his bowl a second time. The noise of purring grew louder. I spread my fingers and pretended to make for Rupert's outstretched neck.

'Don't you touch my cat, Nigel Carlton!' She jumped forward and picked him up in her arms. He managed to keep chewing in mid-air.

'I'd hide your tin-opener next time, that's all I can say.' Thwarted, I leaned round the doorway and hauled the case into the kitchen.

'My suitcase. How kind.'

'Why didn't you ring me from the airport? It could all have been synchronized. You could even have been met by a fully-fed cat.' I glared at Rupert. 'Bloody independent women!'

'Carruthers were paying. They sent me out there, don't forget. Even if it did turn out to be part-work, part-play.'

'How were the Greeks? Still Ancient?'

'They're a very cultured people, Carlton. You wouldn't understand.'

'That's what you said before you went off and left me.'

'You'd have been bored. Parthenon. Mycenae, Epidauros. Terrific, really enjoyed it. Their National Museum was fab, too. Especially their Keeper. Looked like Paul Newman. I now know more about their antiquities than Melina Mercouri.'

'The Keep was the one who forced you into that topless tan, was he?'

'Hotel balcony. Solo,' she told me.

She leaned forward to put the cat back on the floor. 'Delphi was the only place that let me down.'

'Delphi?'

'They've got an oracle there, Dimbo. Only it didn't predict I would be missing all the excitement back at Carruthers & Co. in Bond Street, London.'

I had to think quickly. 'Wouldn't know. Romesh and I have been up north. Tell me.'

'Lucy left it on the Answerphone. Made it sound hilarious, lucky girl. End of big auction. One Arab, dressed like a bank manager, swans into the back shop and pinches half a hundredweight of china just as it's being paid for by another Arab upstairs.'

'I'd have liked to have seen that.' To avoid the green eyes, I bent down and ripped off an airline baggage sticker.

'The one in the suit had a wide-boy East Ender with adenoids in tow. They crammed the whole lot into a filthy old van in five minutes, then buzzed off just as the genuine Son of the Desert comes down the back stairs in his robes to pick it all up. He was not very pleased. They're still trying to sort out the money side, Lucy says. Just my luck to miss all that!'

She walked across the hall and into the bedroom. I threw the scrunched-up sticker at Rupert's head and followed, lugging the suitcase. With a two-handed lift, I dumped the case on the bottom of the bed. In the narrow space between bed and wall, I moved nearer.

Caroline twisted away from me and opened the case. 'I've brought you a present.'

She used the trick to skip past my hands and go back into the kitchen to check on Rupert's progress. He was still eating and purring.

She picked up the Tobermory book I had thrown down when I first came in.

'Not the only one trying to improve myself,' she told me as I returned.

'Romesh is thinking of expanding the Gopal property business. Sudden urge to drop developments and get into Scottish estates. Been reading the price-tags in *Country Life*. Thought I'd better read up about the He-brides.'

'You mean we're going to have "Carlton in the Frozen North"? Wow!' She began flipping pages. 'Why the Spanish Armada to go with it?'

'Eh?'

She put the book back on the work-top. 'That's the one

about 1588 and all that. Spanish galleon blown off course. You *do* realize his chances of buying into gold doubloons are remote?'

She told me the rest of the sad Tobermory story. I filed it away mentally.

'What else did you get up to when I wasn't here, Carlton? In your spare time, I mean.'

'Decided to take up marine biology. Scuby-doo diving.'

'You?'

'I'm very good, thirty feet down. Try me.'

She ignored that. 'Another sudden urge by Gopal & Co., is that it?'

I realized then I had said too much. 'When I totter off on my next lonely hol, I'll be able to check up on the flora, that's all. Do I mean flora? Wildlife.'

It diverted her. 'Fauna,' she told me. 'Anyway, I always thought the wildlife stretched out on the sand was your speciality, Carlton. We can dive as a twosome.'

I pulled her back towards the bedroom.

She wriggled free. 'Let me guess. You want to feel wanted? Your present as tangible proof. That's what you're after.' She stepped away from me. 'Think I rolled it up in my bath-towel.'

She began to push lightweight frocks and underwear to left and right in an elaborate search.

From behind, I slid my hands up and inside her white top. 'It really is an all-over, isn't it?'

'It's here somewhere, your present. You'll like it.' She had to struggle to continue her search. 'Why have you stopped speaking, Nigel Carlton?'

I pulled her gently but firmly towards me.

'I was brought up to beware of Greeks bearing gifts.'

Instead of congratulating me on my grasp of culture, she said, 'Don't do that, I'll flake.' But she twisted herself round and, at short range, began to look at my mouth. It made her green, green eyes cross slightly.

'Carlton Towers, it isn't eight o'clock yet. If you keep doing that, you realize you've got no chance to . . .'

We fell over, sideways.

Rupert trotted into the bedroom, licking his chops and thinking of the duvet. He stopped and looked up at the bed, only to find it was occupied. In a huff, he stalked back towards the kitchen and his empty bowl. Then he mewed.

CHAPTER 6

'Forget Tobermory, Romesh. No way can we plant eighteenth-century Chinese porcelain on a sixteenth-century Spanish warship. Anyway, Caroline says it was cleaned out by hordes of diving Scotsmen. So that's two reasons why we can forget Scotland.' My fingers played with the end of my lurid woollen tie. The present from sunny Greece.

'I shall put Tobermory to one side.'

There was something too calm about the way he said it.

I sat down, squinting into the unexpected English summer sun. 'You'd be better looking at the Scilly Isles. Boats going down there all the time. Local cottage industry, if that's the right phrase.'

'Where precisely in Scotland are Scilly Islands?'

I took a deep breath. 'Off the end of Cornwall, actually.' I thought. 'Romesh, have you spent any time at all reading those books I got you? You've had two whole weeks. They'll be overdue any day, you realize. They whack fines on people.'

'I have spent considerable time reading. I have now pinpointed site of Gopal shipwreck.'

As he said it, I saw on the corner of the desk a new, non-library book. And a new map. Of Scotland. Yet again I had not been consulted. Hurt, I told him, 'I've been busy too, you know. Not just the underwater training. I've also got you the gen on the treasure-hunting gear.'

He was still smirking. 'But first we must know *where* to use such equipment.

'Let me guess. You've already thought of some precise spot.'

He didn't move. 'I can say that "precise spot", as you call it, lies between fifty-seven and one half and fifty-eight and one half degrees North.' He clamped his fingertips together.

'Just give me the name of the place, then.'

'I have selected . . .' Condescending to bend forward at last, he read it out, eyes narrowed. '. . . Island of Lewis. Outer Hebrides.'

'Good God.'

He sat up straight. 'It is very good site. There is much coastline. Many points from which to be more than twelve miles from land.'

'OK, plenty of space for a ship to go down outside the twelve-mile limit. I get the message. You could say ditto for Cornwall. And it's nearer. And warmer.'

'Outer Hebrides are far from attention of media people.'

'I thought you liked the papers?'

'Whole of media is first-class when controlled, Nigel. And control is most easy when they are not there.'

Suddenly he sat up straight again. 'What is most far north-westerly part of British Isles, next to Atlantic Ocean? Next to America?' he demanded.

I felt I was spotlit, in a black leather chair, Magnus

Magnusson staring at me. 'Er, the Outer Hebrides.' I had been helped somewhat.

'Exactly so. Outer Hebrides is most suitable remote place.'

'OK. Now, all of a sudden, you tell me we want peace and quiet. No reptiles from Fleet Street nosing around. Why?'

'We must not have pressmen at start of project, Nigel. At initial dropping of porcelain. Only after exciting find of treasure can we invite.'

I shifted in my chair. The sun was becoming too hot. 'So the democratic decision is Outer Hebrides, is it?'

'Exactly so.' His head waggled horizontally.

'When do we rush up there?'

'You will set off tomorrow, Nigel.'

I was affronted. 'What will *you* be doing?'

'I must concern myself with certain items of survey equipment. And selection of diving crew.'

'I can do that, Romesh. Where do you think I've been for the past fortnight? Buying rounds for my diving instructor.' I re-crossed my legs. 'I'm now a qualified member of the club, you realize!'

That was a mistake—saying 'qualified'.

Romesh stiffened. 'You must not think that qualification is be-all, end-all, Nigel. Lawyers are qualified. Doctors of Medicine are qualified.' He was glaring. 'Chartered Accountants. Surveyors, also.' His face was distorted. He didn't like professional people. They were almost as bad, in his eyes, as tax inspectors or excisemen. Almost.

'You will go north, Nigel.'

'Just because I'm a home-grown Brit, you reckon I know all about bonny bloody Scotland?'

'You know more about than Gopal. I have not been there.' He took a cigar from the Dutch box.

I snorted.

'You will enjoy trip.' He shook out the match and threw it into the elephant's foot.

At last he reached across and unfolded the map. It was the expensive type. I put both hands on the cloth surface and began to search for aeroplane symbols. I found one. 'Think they do daily parachute drops into Stornoway airport?'

But he was already pulling the other large sheet of paper from his middle drawer. 'Critical Path diagram says you will motor to Ullapool.'

I sat up straight. 'If that's what it says, then I'll have to do it.'

'You are being sarcastic once more, Nigel.'

I went back to the map and began another search.

I found Ullapool on the west coast of the mainland, opposite the big island. The print was very small. There was a dotted steamer line leading across to Stornoway. The road north and west from Inverness to Ullapool was a very thin black line.

'It'll take me at least half a day in the MGB.'

As soon as I'd said it, I knew.

'I won't be going by MGB, will I?'

'Van will be necessary to take half porcelain to Far North. In anticipation.' At least he was showing some confidence in my driving abilities. 'Critical Path allows total of one point five days for such action.'

There was something hesitant about it. I craned forward, suspicious. 'Lot of new red writing. All of a sudden.'

He was keeping the work sheet facing his way.

'Nothing else I should be doing while I'm up there, I suppose?' I was struggling to read upside down. The Gopal handwriting made it impossible.

He ticked another line of text. 'You will go to Island of Lewis and select hotel as expedition base-camp.'

'You mean I get to choose? Wow! And how long does it say I'll take to do that tiny extra bit?'

Romesh's finger ran along the red line. 'You have two days, Nigel.'

'Wow! Time to relax.'

He didn't react.

'You'd better show me just where this wreck is,' I told him. 'If you want me to pick out this place.'

He made no move for the map. 'It is between fifty-seven and one half and fifty-eight and one half degrees North.'

I sat up straight. 'You're talking about the whole island, Romesh.'

'I am merely indicating approximate area.'

I put on my John McEnroe face. 'I can not believe this.'

He blinked at me.

'You're not going to tell me the precise spot? Why the hell not?'

'It is better that you . . .'

'I know! The "Need To Know". You think I'll spill the beans as they pour boiling whisky into my left ear. You've been reading too many spy books.' I had to clear my throat. 'I need to know, Romesh. I need to pick out the right hotel.'

'You will choose best hotel on Atlantic shore of island. That will be quite sufficient.'

'You're going to put your comfort before . . .?'

My face must have stayed red. Doubt written on his face, he picked up the new book. It was the Captain Hatcher book on *The Nanking Cargo*. He opened it up at where the slip of paper stuck out. 'I shall give you name of sunken ship, Nigel.'

'Well, thank you very much.' But I felt slightly better.

'It is *De Liefde*. You can read of position in book.' He patted the cover. 'Take with you on trip.'

'Oh yes?'

'But you must not divulge, Nigel! Wild horses must not

drag from you. When in Scotland, you will make pretence of need to survey sea-bottom for oil company. Subterfuge will later persuade pressmen of importance we attach to treasure.' He paused. 'Perhaps I should not after all have told you that . . .'

He closed the book and painfully put his fears to one side. It was too late anyway. He took a deep breath. 'Kindly give me listing of necessary treasure-seeking equipment. I shall acquire while you are in North.' He stubbed out the half-smoked cigar. 'There are one or two further actions I wish you to take.' He bent over the giant double sheet again. I also sighed loudly.

'Take great care, please. And most quietly.' Romesh looked furtively back at the main part of the house. The pile of Chinese crockery he was carrying tilted sharply towards the stack in my arms.

With difficulty, chest heaving, he lowered the fragile soup bowls on to the gravel outside the garage. The armpits of his safari jacket were dark with sweat. Beside him, I too rested, hands on knees.

The sides of the packing cases were starkly white against the stencilled lettering which I had painted on at odd angles. They read: MACHINE PARTS. CARE. Bagha sniffed warily at the new wood.

As a result of that early morning work, my fingers had got completely black. I had been ordered to scrub down. I was still not in the best of moods, having also had to struggle through the London traffic in a hired van with loose brakes. Since I had slept in, my packing of my suitcase had been random. And I had broken one of the tinny locks as I had thrown the case into the back of the van.

Romesh took an armful of straw and bent over to lay it on the bottom of the first empty crate.

'You will lower plates, Nigel. Your arms are longer than

mine. Kindly bear in mind value of each piece.' He picked up half the stack he had brought from the garage. 'Perhaps we should protect each item individually,' he mused.

I snorted and grabbed the blue and white porcelain from him, prodded some straw into the top bowl and dropped the stack, none too gently, into the crate.

'Nigel! These are not motor accessories you are handling now!'

He balanced his stomach on the wooden edge, leaned painfully forward, and pulled the soup bowls out again. Taking more straw and glaring at me, he wound some bits around each soup bowl, then held out the small stack to be re-packed.

The bowls never reached my hands.

'I can't stand watchin' this caper any longer, you two! Here, give them to me, Dad! Nige, pass me that straw.'

She grabbed the stack from her father just as I stretched forward. Her hair peeped from under the pink towel, still wet from the shampoo.

Working at three times our speed, Sharmila filled the whole crate with closely-packed porcelain within five minutes. Her father was allowed to pass across the rest of the straw, I was ordered to ferry the stacks of tableware from the garage.

After two hours, we had completed the whole job. The crates sat, quietly solid, in the back of the van with my suitcase on top.

'Don't forget to bring me back some heather, Nige!' she called out as the van pulled slowly away. I gave a brief wave as I rounded the large, wooden gate-posts and headed for Beckenham High Road and the North.

As soon as I was out of sight, I trod sharply on the accelerator. There was a faint, straw-shrouded noise from behind me. My suitcase slid off one of the crates. It landed on the spare seat and sent the Hatcher book flying on to the floor of the van. The book I had to read to pass away the hours when I had absolutely nothing to do.

CHAPTER 7

'Downtown Ullapool calling London.'

. . .

'Well I can hear *you*, Romesh. Loud and clear.'

. . .

'It should be better, I've just shut two doors. They're having what they call a "wee celebration". Seems to happen every night.'

. . .

'No, everything safe and sound. Made it up here in one day. Positive doddle.'

. . .

'Certainly not. Very carefully. And it's all A-OK, Romesh. All in one piece. Well, two thousand pieces. And safely stored under lock and key in Angus McWilliam's kippering shed. Ex-kippering shed.'

. . .

'Angus says not. He says fish smells don't cling to metal.'

. . .

'Metal. We called them machine parts. Remember?'

. . .

'Right. So I guessed that applied to your porcelain too. Anyway, they'll get washed down in the next few days. And it's very cheap, our mainland base camp. We have the whole shed for twenty-five a month. Plus one litre bottle of Glenfiddich.'

. . .

'Measured the shed up for that already. There's room for

all the survey and pumping gear we care to bring up north. I haven't been idle, exactly.'

. . .

'Right. I was coming to that. Been over there. Rough old trip. Four hours of high teas and high seas. Had to put up with continuous hot air from two travelling salesmen.'

. . .

'Booked us into an hotel on the west coast. Chose it most carefully. Best on the entire west side, they tell me. *Only* one on the west side, actually. But you didn't realize that, did you? When you told me I could choose the best hotel there, Romesh.'

. . .

'No, of course you didn't. Anyway, just beat a pair of Oxford professors to the last two singles. The guests are mostly salmon fishing types.'

. . .

'Place called Valtos.'

. . .

'The Loch Roag Arms, actually.'

. . .

'That's right, but different spelling. Looks just what you wanted. Two hours' hard driving over a hairy road due west out of Stornoway. Only road, in fact. Anyway, out in front of the place there's a view of one hundred nautical miles of North Atlantic. Plus one island right in the middle distance, just as you ordered. Hope you're satisfied, Romesh. We're not going to find another in a hurry. Just a minute.'

. . .

'Had to borrow more coins.'

. . .

'No, I didn't play it exactly that way. Wasn't on.'

. . .

'I know that's what you told me to do, Romesh, but—'

. . .

'If you'll let me get a word in, Romesh—'

. . .

'Thank you. I've booked a boat direct from the hotel bod over there instead. A nice little number. Converted trawler.'

. . .

'Because in the first place there weren't any so-called "support vessels" here in Ullapool. Or any other type of boat for hire. That was why. Plus the thought occurred that doing it that way we wouldn't have another boat puttering after us every morning as we went out into the broad Atlantic.'

. . .

'No problem. He'd welcome the break from keeping inns, he said. Which means that, as soon as we get to Ullapool with the other half of our stuff, William John Macleod, proprietor of the Loch Roag Arms, will begin to chunter across the Minch in what he calls his *Girl Mairi* and we load everything on to it.'

. . .

'No. He'll pilot us back through the Sound of Harris and half way up the west coast of the island to Valtos. All he needs, he reckons, is a bell from Ullapool telling him we've arrived up here and he'll come across.'

. . .

'Right. I'll tell him he can stop counting beds and start greasing up the engine of his boat.'

. . .

'Forty-five feet long. Black, with gold trim. One owner. Top speed, fifteen knots. Five thousand on the clock. You'll like William John. He's fond of his dram, too.'

. . .

'His whisky.'

. . .

'It doesn't get dark up here until after nine. Amazing.

We'll be able to work fifteen-hour days, I reckon. If we can
stand up in the wind. And keep dry.'

. . .

'I was coming to that. You said I had to do it discreetly,
right? They've already started to take me for the scout of a
heavy survey expedition. That's right. In both Highland
beauty-spots. Scouting for oil, I've already got them thinking. The boys here were much impressed by the crates. And
when I dropped something into our chat about sea-bottom
readings, it made The McWilliam put down his glass of
Glenfiddich very smartly. Now I get called "Captain
Carlton" on every Ullapool street corner—by people I've
never seen before. Whole town seems to know.'

. . .

I stopped to take in air. 'In fact, there's only been one
real embarrassment all the time I've been up here, Romesh.'

. . .

'Try to guess.'

. . .

'No, I *know* the name of the wreck. Not that I'm telling
anyone. Not at this stage. It's the exact spot on the bed of
the ocean where our deep-frozen Dutchman lies that I'm
talking about, Romesh.'

. . .

'A good reason why? Ye gods! Whether I'm a fake oil-man
or a real treasure-hunter, I needed to look at something
fairly fixed. I looked a real English twit over in the bloody
Loch Roag Arms, scanning the horizon through a whole
one hundred and eighty degrees instead of staring at
one particular chunk of sea. Macleod didn't look all that
impressed, Romesh.'

. . .

'Yes,. I did read the Hatcher book. On the ferry-boat
going over there. You were having me on, weren't you?
They don't know exactly where the bloody Dutchman did

go down in seventeen-hundred and whatever! Could have been any place between Anglesey and the Shetlands. So how come *you* know, Romesh? How come you know that it went down within spitting distance of the Loch Roag Arms, Valtos, Isle of Lewis?'

. . .

I moved the receiver to my other ear. 'Romesh, I need to know. Tell me exactly where the hell this sunken wreck of yours is!'

. . .

My voice grew tighter. 'No, you have not already told!'

. . .

'Jesus Christ!'

I slammed down the receiver. Then I threw open the door to the tiny booth and stomped back through the second door, into the bar. I ordered a double malt.

He was bending over the billiard table, about to play a cannon, when I marched in.

'You let me go all the way up there! Like some lame-brain!' I crashed my case down on his parquet. He made the shot.

'And the minute I've finished every damned thing off up there, you tell me that you don't know where the real wreck is. That you've had a better idea. That you're building it down here. Jesus!'

Romesh chalked his cue. 'It is better for overall control of media. And so much easier. Were we not having difficulty in finding suitable wrecked vessel in library books?'

He leaned over the green baize, sized up his next shot, but then straightened up. He must have sensed my tightening jawline.

'Concept came to me during last game. Just after you had driven off. I asked myself: Why do we not come up with own sunken galleon? It is wrong verb, but you understand. Would you like to play?'

I ignored the offer.

'You knew where I was. You could have rung me before I left Ullapool to go hotel-hunting on that effing island.'

He played the shot. The red ball slipped into a bottom pocket.

'Lack of complete knowledge allowed you to resemble genuine oil-man to people in hotel, Nigel.'

Now I knew the real reason.

He straightened up. 'And your concept of hiring support vessel from hotel-owner himself was very good, Nigel. Very good.'

Feeling slightly better, I put the ball back on its spot for him.

'And how do you propose to build it? Going to Upper Clyde Shipbuilders?'

That was the moment when the next couple of days turned really rocky.

'It is already in hands. In hands of Gopals. They are constructing necessary section of hull.' He tried a long cannon, off three cushions.

'Section of hull?'

'It is not necessary to do more. Part only of hull will be sufficient to appear in video.' His white ball just missed the other white.

'Video?'

'It is most essential module of whole deceit. We must show media people—and auction house—dramatic moment when porcelain is found, then retrieved, from wreck. We need props. We require part of ancient hull, but only as backdrop, you understand.'

He put his cue back on the rack.

'I have already instructed Gopal artisans. They have been

asked to copy exactly illustration of Dutch merchant vessel from book.'

'Artisans?'

He turned out the lights above the table and opened the curtains, eyes narrowed in the sudden sunlight. 'Artisans. People who produce artefacts, Nigel.'

'I must now arrange cameraman. I have not yet had time to telephone Rolf. You see, it has been constant activity since you left.'

I looked pointedly at the billiard balls and snorted.

We walked out of the panelled room, Romesh slightly ahead. Going back into the den, he flopped down in his favourite chair and prodded telephone digits with a stubby finger.

'Rolf? Romesh Go—'

As I sat down, I overheard Rolf Hostler finish off the Gopal surname for him.

'I am eager to use Hostler Enterprises skills, Rolf. I require video cameraman. Skilled. Able to compose shots also.'

I whispered, 'Underwater,' across the desk.

Romesh did not look up. 'To work unsupervised, without director, you understand.'

'Able to swim,' I hissed at him.

'It would be advantageous if he were able to travel. We require services for one week in northern Scotland. Rolf, it is exciting prospect.'

He let the sentence hang.

'There is Scotsman available?' exclaimed Romesh. 'But that is most opportune! Kindly ask him to present himself at earliest hour tomorrow. In Beckenham. Concerning payment . . .'

The metallic voice grew stronger. 'He's self-employed, Romesh. You'll find out it's better that way. Best of luck on the expedition. Stag-hunting, is it? Anyway, I'll get Archie to pack plenty of lens covers. To keep off the rain.'

'For once, Rolf, there is no need to rent camera from you. I shall provide. Sharmila has been most generous on my birthday. It is just that I do not trust myself on first hand-held camera outing.' He winked at me. 'We require only cameraman.'

Romesh put back the receiver. 'That is commencement of media aspects,' he told me.

'Romesh, you said nothing to him about the shooting being underwater.'

'I am using "Need to Know" basis.'

'Right.'

He still looked bland. 'It is not necessary for Rolf Hostler to know of complete scenario. Only cameraman should be so informed. And at last moment.'

'So what about the optical gear? You're going to need special stuff. Waterproof casings; that sort of thing.'

'It is already considered. While you were in north of Scotland, I have gathered together complete inventory of search equipment. And photographic items also. Still camera, video devices, rubberized lighting. It is all stored in garage awaiting your attention.' He tilted back his chair and puffed out his large chest. 'I have even remembered scuba equipment—which was not on Carlton listing. I have been comprehensive. You will be surprised.'

'I've already been surprised.' I stared at him.

It had no effect.

'It is also vital that we have documentary proof of porcelain which we will be telling people was on East Indiaman.'

I frowned at him.

'Shipping papers to show to trusting auction people and buying public that porcelain travelled from Canton ware-house on doomed vessel.'

He put his hands behind his head and lay back in the chair.

'I have had to take up intellectual challenge in composing imaginary ship's manifest. List of items on board, Nigel.'

'Don't forget the auction boys are used to poring over ancient manuscripts. See them every day.'

It didn't work.

The hands stayed behind head. 'Cousin Mohan has found me completely blank piece of paper from eighteenth century. Or so. It is advantage of antiques trade. Many bureau drawers with untouched items still inside.'

'Let me guess the next bit. You've got an aged Gopal uncle who just happens to be able to forge the odd—'

'Youngest son of Mohan has completed Italic writing competition at grammar school. Second prizeman. He has welcomed opportunity to use newly-acquired calligraphy. We shall have convincing document.'

'You seem to have done it all. I could have stayed where I was. Not bothered to drive back from Ullapool. Rested up.'

If he spotted the sarcasm, he gave no sign. 'We shall need great driving skills to take second instalment of porcelain —and rest of equipment to Far North.' He looked earnest.

Things were looking up.

'I have also arranged for some help in other aspect of your activity.'

'Oh yes?'

'You will need others to dive with you.'

'Romesh, I don't see—'

He held up his hand.

'It has been taken care of already. Captain Hatcher used full diving team in South China Sea to locate real treasure in real ship. Auction house people will expect us also to have experience in warmer waters of treasure pursuit.'

Something was coming. I just didn't know what it was.

'Right,' I said, very slowly.

'Exactly so.' Romesh waggled his head. 'And you will not therefore be surprised if other members of diving team have exotic appearance.' He was only just stopping himself laughing.

I got there. My shoulders fell back against the zebra-skin.

'Don't tell me, Romesh. You've set me up with The Diving Gopals.'

I got up out of the chair.

With my own improved cash-flow over the last three years, I have moved out of half a room into two, plus loo and an overgrown alcove where somebody could possibly cook things. It is centrally-heated. It is near Sloane Square. It needs dusting. But it means I am close to Caroline's pad. And vice-versa.

She stood in front of the open, battered suitcase and almost threw the hat back inside. She had arrived at my flat ten minutes early. Which had had at least one advantage. She had got there just before I would have taken my new, expensive wetsuit from the cupboard and thrown it on top of all the other travelling items.

'I could see it in your little face, Carlton! The disappointment when I told you the *Tobermory* was now as empty as yesterday's bowl of porridge.'

She turned to face me. 'Scotched your plan, eh?'

She stuck out her tongue. 'And you didn't really expect me to believe all that bull about marine biology, did you?'

She drew a finger along the mantelpiece, then looked at the tip.

'I still don't see why you think I would be going to Scotland to look for gold.'

'Because you're transparent, Carlton, that's why! First, you disappear for two whole days without a word. *Then*, as soon as you get back, you announce you'll be gone again.

To some unspecified place. In August. And I find you packing wool shirts and pullovers. And *this*.'

At last she threw the deerstalker. It landed on top of the jumble of clothes.

'It's got to be Scotland, hasn't it? And it's got to be something villainous—otherwise you'd have blabbed about it already.'

'I've told you, woman. Rubbish is really into Scottish estates. Smitten by the thought of owning large tracts of grouse moor. That's all there is to it.'

'Why doesn't he get hitched again?' She often went off on tangents.

'Eh?'

'He's had time to get over it. How long's he been a widower now?'

'He's perfectly set-up as he is. Who needs to get married?'

She made a face before she spoke. 'Rattling around in that huge ark with just one punk daughter to keep him happy?'

'Are you suggesting incest in the—?'

'Shut up, Carlton. You have a dirty mind. All I'm saying is that he should get married again. It's not healthy. And so should she—instead of mooching around with a Hindustani crush on the hired help!'

I slammed the case shut, not just to change the subject but to pretend it was ready for travel. The broken lock snapped open again.

'Just business? No dullskuggery? No nipping off to peer into the murky waters of Tobermory Bay in case they left a doubloon in the mud?'

I put on my honest look. 'No gold-digging, if that's what you mean.'

'And no gold-diggers?'

'No way.' I moved closer and slid both hands round her waist.

'So when will you be back?'

'Not long.' I found a zip.

'How long is "Not long", Carlton?'

'Maybe a couple of weeks.' I saw her face. 'Ten days. It'll take that to finalize any deals with the legal mafia up there.'

Caroline zipped her skirt up and stepped round me. 'Then you can make love to me at that point in time.' She smiled over-sweetly. 'When I'm more convinced of your motives. All of them. Makes sense, doesn't it?'

'I'll phone you.'

'You'll send me a card, Carlton. At least three lines long.'

'I tell you I'm going up to Scotland with my boss. The man who pays me. To improve my knowledge of estate management. It's a career move, woman.'

She picked up her red umbrella. 'I wish you would. Move your career.'

'He pays well. Very well. And it's exciting. How many other employers would give me the chance to travel . . .'

She was looking deep into my eyes. 'With your looks and charm, Nigel Carlton, you could make it in the City. Or a car dealership. You've got all it takes.'

As she stepped across the room and I followed, she drew the cold end of the stumpy umbrella gently down my nose. 'I could even see you selling porcelain from the Carruthers podium . . .'

'To distraught A-rabs?'

'If only you'd let me take you in hand!'

'Why do you think I invited you round here, woman?'

She stuck out her tongue again and shut my own door in my face.

CHAPTER 8

There was no room in my normal parking place. I had to walk across a long stretch of gravel. The thin brown man had one leg buckled under his body, the other stretched out against the biggest curved upright. The long, bare toes held on to the wood as he chipped away with the adze. It was part of the hull of a boat. They had almost finished.

The older brown man looked up from his hand-drill and showed me his blackened teeth in a wide grin. 'Fresh worm-holes, sahib.'

I said, 'Bloody hell,' to myself and crunched on, towards the sunlit front door.

I expected some resistance to my shove. As the door jerked backwards, I tottered into the cool hall.

'Come away in, Mr Carlton! Good morning to you!'

The stocky little man grinned from the darkness. In the other hand he had a brimming glass of whisky. He pushed a lank piece of black hair back from his brow.

'Archie, Archie Gallacher. We'll be workin' together, you and me. So don't forget I'll have you dead in my sights!' I hadn't noticed the viewing device until Gallacher pulled the lanyard off his outsize belly and put it to one small eye.

'Sorry?'

'Sights. This wee gadget has seen service in a lot of war zones, Mr Carlton, let me tell you.'

'Sorry?'

'War zones, Mr Carlton. Nigel. Archie.'

He started to wave the glass, then decided to lower the level of whisky instead. 'Rolfie told me you're the one doin' the drivin', so I won't offer you one o' these, eh?'

Behind him, I heard the noise of the study door. Sharmila

walked past the archway, looked in to give me an exclusive smile, and walked on towards the kitchen. She was suddenly walking faster.

'Hello, hen!' Gallacher called after her.

Silence.

He took another hefty drink. 'That's a lassie with a classy chassis you've got on tap there, Nigel my boy.' He aimed a dig at my ribs. I stepped back.

All at once he spoke in a posh Edinburgh accent. 'Just lead me to my instruments of artistry in your own good time, my man. I'm happy to wait till you're quite ready.'

I left him sitting in the deepest armchair. Archie was looking up at the sun through the cut-glass side of the best Gopal Waterford crystal.

I needed to see him urgently. I pushed open the study door without waiting to knock.

'Romesh, you don't expect me to work alongside that, do you? I can only understand forty per cent. And that sounds like bull. One hundred per cent.'

He tipped the sagging cigar ash into the elephant's foot and waved me to the chair. I stayed in front of the desk.

I had more to tell him. 'He's only offering round your whisky. He's only starting to sexually harass your only daughter. By the time we set out today, that bod out there is going to be completely p-i-s-s-e-d.'

For something to do, I moved the cigar box six inches right and shut the lid. 'I have two solid days of Highland accents, and now you produce five feet three of pure Glasgow. Send him back. Haven't we got a "sale or return" set-up with Hostler? We give him enough business.'

Romesh put both elbows on the blotter and laced his fingers.

'It is camera skills we require, Nigel. I have already telephoned this morning. When I discovered that I also could not comprehend. Rolf is insistent, however. We have top cameraman in Mr Gallacher.'

I snorted and walked towards the window, past his chair.

'It is case of acquiring taste, perhaps.'

'He's the one acquiring the taste. Have you seen the level of your decanter lately?'

I marched past him a second time, back to my own side of the desk.

'Let me suggest, Nigel, that you busy yourself in inventory. In garage.' He said it soothingly.

I was struggling to read my own writing. The entry on the dog-eared list I'd left with Romesh had been over-written in that strange Indian script. I got on to one knee to look at the piece of survey gear on the garage floor.

'Hey, that's magic. Look at a' them goodies!' Archie came in and balanced one thick crepe sole on the oxygen cylinder I had just ticked off.

'I was just thinkin', Nigel boy. You could drop me off for a while as we tool through Coatbridge. You know, slow down to thirty-five on a corner and I'll roll out o' the van. See the missus. When do you really need me up there in the Arctic Circle?'

I thought fast. 'Not for a good few days.'

'So where exactly is this biblical epic bein' shot, then?'

'The Outer Hebrides.'

'Oh my God.'

'Lewis.'

'Isn't that an island? I'd have to catch a boat. On my own.'

I gave a quick nod, keen to get through the list.

'On second thoughts, Nigel boy, forget the Big Drop-off.'

Archie lowered the broad, blue shoe.

'So where's all my Cecil B. de Mille stuff, then?'

I pointed absent-mindedly at the waterproofed video equipment.

He lifted up the camera in horror.

'What is this? A new-fangled silencer or somethin'?'

'Underwater casing. Good for thirty-five fathoms,' I told him, seeing his face for the first time.

'Is that a fact? Thirty-five fathoms? Under the water, eh?'

With his half-empty glass, Gallacher retreated to the back of the garage and sat silently on a packing case while I worked on.

It was when I'd got to the second-last entry that I had my other worrying thought.

I finished off the list, then slid the scaffolding poles back along the concrete floor. Just then, Romesh came in, flashed a vague smile towards Archie, and stood looking proudly down at the neatly-stacked equipment. He put one hand in the pocket of his safari suit and jangled his keys.

'Romesh, just who is going to operate all these high-tech nautical surveying what's-its?'

'I have not told?'

'You have not told. No.'

He looked at a hairy wrist. 'I have instructed Mr Hagemann to be with us not later than twelve o'clock noon. He will not let us down. He is most impressive person.'

At that point I decided to delay telling him about my other worry. About the working experience of our cameraman.

We both swung round at the sound of high heels on gravel.

'Dad. This is Mervyn, Dad.'

I'd never heard her breathless before. Not after a twenty-five-yard journey from her front door.

As her father chatted to the smooth and sleek arrival, Sharmila sidestepped. She spoke without taking her eyes off the newcomer.

'Wow, Nige!' she said quietly out of the side of her mouth.

I thought he looked over-dressed. The hair was probably back-combed. The thin moustache was definitely hyper-trim. It was even being stroked as he spoke to her father.

Romesh turned.

'Nigel, allow me to introduce you to Mr Mervyn Hagemann. He will be resident expert in all things electronic. He is also most familiar with boats. And most experienced diver.'

I shook the hand as soon as it moved down from the upper lip. To my disappointment, the grip was very firm.

For the next few minutes, I didn't know what was said or done. The stranger looked and behaved too like the young Robert Taylor in a late-night movie re-run.

I was vaguely aware of being left on my own.

The noises were coming from the study. I could hear the deep Hagemann voice and, even more often, Romesh saying, 'Exactly so.'

I went quietly back to the garage and started to think about the job of loading up.

'Exactly so. I shall talk to Nigel.' The growing noise came from the corridor.

I looked up.

'We must follow precisely Mr Hagemann's advice, Nigel. We must have paper read-out from scanning device already pre-prepared. To show interesting sea-bed images. It will be work of moments for him to produce, he assures me.'

I stared.

'He will require equipment handbook for study on journey north, Nigel.' He held out his hand.

'Brilliant! While you two creative people are discussing theory, I'll just busy myself with the artisan bits and bobs.'

I shoved the plastic-wrapped manual at him.

'Don't worry. Mr Gallacher and I can easily handle the

heavy stuff. No need for you or Herr Hagemann to attend. Not at all. And I'll make sure we don't stash away any of your woodworkers, as we pack up the hull.'

I had guessed right. In his excitement, he had forgotten his own carpenters.

'I shall leave in your safe hands, Nigel.'

'Exactly so,' I told him.

'Nige. What a dish! Wow! Think he's got a girlfriend?'

Sharmila poured my coffee into and over the rim of my large brown mug.

'Gallacher? Terrific bloke.'

'You know who I'm on about, Nige!'

'Merv the Magician? Bit worried about the 'tache,' I told her. 'Could mean homosexual tendencies. He's already given the hall mirror a bashing.'

'You've gone bright green, Nige! Really green!'

'I think I'd rather have Wee Archie.'

At that point Gallacher came in. He balanced his empty glass on the end of the work-top and began to waggle his bean-bag bottom on to the high stool next to me. He put both hands to his chin and smiled a huge smile at Sharmila.

'Coffee for Little Me?'

She turned away and got out a chocolate biscuit for me. A thing she'd never done before.

Romesh came in. Sharmila poured out his coffee before he had reached his seat.

'Nigel, you and Mr Gallacher here have done excellently. Mr Hagemann has confirmed that everything is securely packed away.'

'Good, good. That's excellent, isn't it, Archie?'

Gallacher nodded, without moving his pleading gaze away from Sharmila.

Romesh took one sip.

'We are almost ready. I have just one—'

'Dad, I've just given Madhu a bell. She can come over to feed Bagha startin' tomorrow. She—'

'You will stay here until called upon, young lady. You will come to Scotland at head of diving team.'

'I've given them the map, Dad. They're quite happy. Find their way easily, they said. And they don't want a woman cloggin' up their Dormobile.'

'You are not to be with us in vanguard, Sharmila.' Romesh was straight-faced. He hadn't seen his pun.

Hagemann strode into the kitchen.

'I know what is it that is going through your mind,' Romesh told his daughter.

Sharmila produced a bone-china cup and saucer from a top shelf for her latest arrival and poured carefully. After Hagemann had taken his first sip and shown her his perfect teeth, she gave Gallacher his coffee in my old mug. The one with the chipped rim.

We were ready to go north.

Just as I went through the hall for the last time, I stumbled painfully over a padlocked hold-all on the mat. I tried to throw it to one side. It was amazingly heavy.

'It is wearing apparel.' I hadn't heard Romesh's feet. 'You have said northern weather is most unpredictable, Nigel.'

I grunted in disbelief. He took the bag from me.

'Also one or two personal artefacts. To bring total profit to round figure. I shall explain later.' He disappeared towards the van.

I knew the phrase. It meant I would not find out for some time.

We were all aboard. Romesh leaned out to say goodbye.

'Dad?' Her voice was plaintive.

'I have told. It is not possible. You will await.'

She turned and fled back into the house.

I started the engine.

Suddenly Romesh hit the dashboard with the flat of his hand. 'Supply of tea, Nigel! I have omitted.'

I said, 'I thought you and Mr Hagemann had—'

'It is most important prop. Sharmila will provide.'

The voice came from the second row of seats. 'Leave it to me, Nigel boy. I used to be a caddy back in Scotland.' He paused. 'Get it?'

Nobody laughed.

I thought I heard the hall toilet flush. Round the corner of the house, Archie came towards us, his short arms round a half-box of tea, stamped ASSAM. He was already out of breath.

'You should have told me, Mr Gopal. I'd have packed my golf trolley for the trip.'

We drove past the front of the house, leaving Sharmila to wave tearfully from the wide doorstep. Bagha barked once.

Nobody said anything inside the van until we reached the main road. Romesh struggled to master the folds of the road-map.

Gallacher spoke. 'Did I ever tell you gents about the time I was shot up in Beirut?'

CHAPTER 9

I had enjoyed the first trip north. And I reckoned that the company now with me would make the second journey even more pleasant. By the fourth junction of the M1 nobody had spoken a word to me.

I stared at the reflection of Hagemann. It was deeply into the manual for our side-scan sonar. Every glossy page made an irritating swish as he flicked it over. And he had lit up his pipe. I thought he looked pathetic.

Further back in the van, wedged between the crates of porcelain and the survey and diving gear, Gallacher had started to paw over the contents of his plastic bag. One of the cans rolled aimlessly across the metal floor. That also annoyed me. And Romesh was reading too.

I overtook a juggernaut, then looked sideways. 'Interesting book? Read out the juicy bits and we can all laugh and joke.'

Romesh solemnly read on to the end of the paragraph before he looked up, over his half-moon spectacles. 'It is concerning John Brown. It is serious subject. And most intriguing.'

'This isn't the Mason-Dixon Line we're heading for, Romesh. It's M1, M6, then the Scottish border.'

'I am savouring story of Queen Victoria. She set highest store by honesty of Scottish retainer, John Brown. It is excellent omen.'

'She just liked bare knees, Romesh. Kilts, sporrans. That sort of stuff. Didn't see one all the time I was up there.'

There was a sudden sharp hiss.

'No, thank you kindly,' Romesh said over his shoulder to Gallacher's outstretched beer-can.

'What is it, Mr Romesh? The religion? OK. They don't play 4-3-4 formation where you come from, do they? Travelled, see. Still globe-trottin', as a matter of fact.' Archie waved the can and read out the label. 'Czechoslovakia.' He reached into his plastic bag and pulled out two more. 'Belgium. Denmark,' he announced. 'Tomorrow the World!' He dropped the cans back. He started to whistle. Badly.

I stretched across and pushed in my cassette. The sounds of the Jimmie Lunceford Band, 1937, playing 'He ain't got

Rhythm' filled the van. Romesh winced; he always did when
I play jazz. Behind me, I could just hear Hagemann grunt
at some obscure technical point as he rattled the pipe stem
against his perfect teeth.

I swung the wheel left to turn into a motorway restaurant.
It was still dark. It had begun to rain.

Almost all the other people in the queue had spilled
numbly out of an overnight coach. The line of pale faces
stared at the prose of the spotted menu and tried to decide
between the Super-Brit Breakfast and the Gettysburger
Authentic Brunch. The prices also looked unreal. It was
1.30 a.m.

Gallacher was the only one to turn down coffee. Hoping
to shame him, I picked out Highland Spring, carbonated.
He ignored the bottle as it lay beside him at the table.
Nobody spoke.

For the rest of the night I drove on through the intermittent
lighting of the motorways. By the Liverpool turn-off, Romesh's head lay on the lapels of his safari suit and the
Hagemann pipe had stopped glowing. And just south of
Preston, Gallacher exhausted his supply of off-key whistling.
The wandering tin of lager gave off an emptier note as it
rolled.

We sped through the Scottish border country as dawn
broke. The M74 was less busy than before. The wet surface
of the new road system skirting Glasgow shone in the early
morning sunlight.

There was a sudden sharp rattle from behind. 'Hey? What
happened to the border, son?' Gallacher lurched forward
on to his knees and squinted over Romesh's sleeping
shoulder into the light of the new day. He narrowed his eyes
to read a road-sign. 'Jesus Christ, we've gone by it! Have
you no soul?'

'Tried to waken you.'

'Is that so? What did you use? Some o' them Public School vowels of yours, I suppose.' He burped. 'That accent o' yours needs a cure, Nigel my boy. Here, grab some cough mixture.' He pushed the can of Stella Artois at me. 'I'd rather you had it than Einstein here. At least you're doin' some o' the work.'

As I shook my head, Gallacher nodded towards the sleeping Hagemann. Then he began to read out every passing road-sign.

After twenty more minutes the two of us were staring up at Stirling Castle.

'Uphill all the way now, Nigel boy! Into Big Sky Territory!' Gallacher tightened his tie. 'Came here once. Celtic. Away. Beat their Albion in the third round.' He lost his happy expression. 'Last town in the Lowlands. Oxygen debt from now on, old son.' He shivered, then drained the can. 'Never mind, let's look on the bright side, eh? Realize this place never fell to the English? Never.' He waved the empty beer-can at the disappearing ramparts. 'Hardly ever.' He began to hum 'A Scottish Soldier.'

Romesh started to snore again. And the sonar manual slipped from the Hagemann knee. Gallacher began to find the names of the Highland towns difficult to pronounce.

The air was becoming ever brighter, thinner, sharper. Romesh woke up. I could see in the mirror that Hagemann had picked up the manual again and was pretending that he hadn't been asleep. He tapped the bowl of his pipe against the metal wall of the van.

The road-signs told us how to leave the A9 to reach Braemar, Dee-side, Balmoral. I swerved round a kilted cyclist struggling in a high gear. 'Probably a Royal,' I told a yawning Romesh. He straightened up, peered out, then slumped.

But it had worked. He was now fully awake. 'We must

unload equipment with obvious effort. Only transfer of hull
and of stored porcelain will be surreptitiously done,' he told
me.

'I packed my bedroom slippers.' I was beginning to feel
the effects of my drive.

'Nigel, perhaps Mr Hagemann should now take over
driv—'

He saw my knuckles whiten on the wheel. I trod on the
accelerator.

'Very well. But remember when we arrive at destination.
It would be bad form to motor hundreds of miles only to
fall at first hurdle.'

'I thought this was a van, not a—' But it was lost.

'Where is this?' Romesh stared out at the panorama.

'The Beauly Firth. Inverness. You could nip in and buy
Sharmila a pair of tartan trews.'

He looked suddenly prim.

'Slacks for ladies,' I explained. 'Just give them your
surname and they'll tell you which clan you belong to. I'm
a McAllister.'

'My God. Aberdeen.' Gallacher had woken up and misread
the large green and white sign.

'Inverness,' I told him. 'Gateway to the Islands.'

'Indian territory,' said our Scotsman. He felt the stare.
'Red Indian Territory, Mr Romesh. Red Indian.' Unap-
preciated, he struggled to the back of the van again.

Romesh nodded towards him 'Do you think . . .?' he
began to ask me quietly.

'His first time this far north. You're not alone.'

But Gallacher wasn't finished. 'My God, what a throat!'

I passed the big plastic bottle across my left shoulder.

'Never touch the stuff, Nigel. Water and me don't get on.'

Romesh and I exchanged looks.

'I'll hang on till we get into Glen Fiddich.'

'That was half an hour ago.'

'Right, Nigel boy, OK. You're the Trail Boss.' He stayed where he was, an elbow on the back of each front seat. The smell of stale beer hit me.

We zipped over the road-bridge at Kessock, heading for the fertile soil of the Black Isle.

Someone grunted behind Gallacher's shoulders. I saw another cloud of tobacco smoke in the mirror and wound down the window. We pulled up for each of us to go behind his individual tree in the last clump of pines before the high bare ground after Strathpeffer.

All at once Loch Broom appeared, long and thin, over the snub nose of the van. Beyond we could see the steel-blue waters of the Minch. And between the two colours of water, the little town of Ullapool pointed a white-painted fingernail towards the western side of the loch.

We passed a black and white sign which read '*Failte gu Ulapul*'.

I said, 'It's either "Welcome to Ullapool", or "Sassenachs Keep Out". Something like that.' I had to explain the word Sassenachs to Romesh.

Wearily I pulled up in the hotel car-park. The equipment in the rear slid one inch towards Hagemann. Gallacher was first out, heading towards the sign reading 'Gents'.

Throwing my case on the bed, I picked up the telephone and asked the soft Highland voice to get me a Stornoway number.

CHAPTER 10

The next morning's light was just as bright.

Behind the rest of us, Archie Gallacher slapped his hands together and shivered.

'God's Own Country,' he announced. 'Land of the Free
. . . Kirk.' Then he stopped in mid-stride. He was staring
past us, down towards the harbour.

'Don't tell me that is it. Tell me that is not it, Nigel boy.'

He had seen what was moored at the jetty. The bow said
Girl Mairi.

'You will be Mister Gopal.' The voice from the little
wheelhouse was emphatic but soft, softer than I remembered. 'Mister Carlton was telling me all about you. Except
what exactly you are in the islands to do.'

The big man with the high red cheekbones winked at us
and skipped off the bobbing deck on to the thick planks of
the jetty. He looked even more like a displaced Viking. He
wiped his hands on the gigantic oatmeal polo-neck. The
eyes were sparkling. And behind the pinpoints of light there
was something shrewd.

'Fresh over from the Loch Roag this morning, gentlemen.
Just like the fish. I am glad to meet with you. And to offer
you all a warm welcome.'

Before Romesh could reply, he shouted out, 'Jump on
board now, gentlemen! Jump on board!' The slow accent
made the words sound like 'chump' and 'chentlemen'.

The big man guided a wide-eyed Romesh from the
squeaky but solid planking on to the moving deck. 'Just so
long as you are not planning to turn yourselves into White
Settlers, if you follow me, Mr Gopal.'

My boss looked upset as they shook hands. Romesh got his
hand back at last. I could see him try to waggle blood back
into the paralysed fingers.

'What I am meaning is the people who come up here and
buy a property, Mr Gopal. To buy holiday homes for
themselves. But we call them the White Settlers. Or worse.'
The great head came nearer to Romesh's ear. 'And as an
hotel-man, I like them even less than the other islanders do.
Taking the bread from my mouth.' He snorted. 'And only

to see their backs every September and their new green
wellingtons on the very next May Day.'

He planted a hand on Romesh's shoulder. 'A legacy of
the colonial past. But you will appreciate that, coming from
the sub-continent as you do. We will be sharing a certain
solidarity, Mr Gopal.'

Romesh, still looking baffled, stepped forward.

Hagemann and I jumped just after them, on to the patch
of deck they had left. Hagemann was the one who didn't
slip, of course.

There was not enough room in the wheelhouse for us all.

Pretending to follow the path of Hagemann's pipe as it
swept the sea-loch, I could just catch the odd word.

'Uganda . . . Lake Victoria . . . Subject peoples . . . Solidarity.'

Romesh was sounding as if he had recovered his inner
calm. Beside me, Hagemann coughed happily and tamped
down his tobacco.

The door of the wheelhouse opened. '. . . is what you'll
be wondering, Mr Gopal. It is because I'm a Macleod.
William John Macleod. Like two hundred other men on the
Isle of Lewis. So a nickname is not a luxury but a necessity.
"Galore" it will be for me from now on and we will get on
fine.'

At last, Gallacher jumped. He landed half on a hawser,
wobbled wild-armed, and swore. Galore caught the flailing
right hand in his own and pulled him upright. He didn't let
go. I introduced them hurriedly.

'From Glasgow, is it, Mr Gallacher?' The voice was no
longer soft. '*Ciamar a tha thu?*'

Gallacher's jaw dropped.

Satisfied, Galore turned to Romesh and me. 'The Gaelic,
you see. You will all be needing a transfusion of the language
before this boat reaches Valtos pier. It will oil wheels on
the island, you understand. For whatever is going to be your

mischief, Mr Gopal.' The eyes had become even shrewder.

Galore pulled a book from his hip pocket. The stained and warped cover said *Gaelic without Groans*.

'I keep this for my English clients.' Galore flipped to a middle page. 'Take this phrase now, gentlemen.' He held it up for us all to see. 'How would you say this, now?'

Romesh peered, then read out the line of print slowly and phonetically. 'S-l-a-i-n-t-e M-h-a-t-h,' he said.

Galore turned and leaned back inside the wheelhouse. The hand now held a half-empty whisky bottle.

'Well now, what they do not say in the books is that you should miss out one letter for every three Gaelic ones that are written down. Then you would be nearer the truth.' He paused to let it sink in. 'I would pronounce what you have just said as "Slan'che Va", Mr Gopal.' His sudden grin was full of gold teeth. 'It means "Good Health", Mr Gopal. But what they say is that nobody can appreciate such a message without a dram inside them.'

He lifted the bottle to his mouth and drank. Then he wiped the top and passed it to Romesh. '*Slainte Mhath* to you, Mr Gopal!'

Romesh slowly took a swig. Suddenly he looked better.

The huge tanned hand took the bottle from him and set it back on the narrow shelf just inside the wheelhouse.

Galore closed the textbook and stuffed it back in his trousers. 'But there's other training to get through first, is there not? Now, who is to be your captain, Mr Gopal? Who is to be the master of my beautiful *Girl Mairi*?'

Romesh looked round and beckoned. Hagemann stepped past me and gripped Galore's hand. The big man looked impressed.

'Capital. A man with a firm grip for the wheel. We are already half way there, so to speak.' The two men went into the wheelhouse.

The others stepped back on to the jetty, Gallacher ahead of Romesh and me.

'What is meaning of "Galore"?' Romesh whispered.

'Title of a book. And an old Ealing flick. Full name *Whisky Galore*.'

All at once Romesh looked as if something had been made clearer to him.

'Remember oil pretence,' he hissed.

'Oil pretence,' I muttered, and rolled up my sleeves.

All that morning and into the early afternoon, Gallacher and I worked away in the McWilliam shed, with some lightweight help from Romesh. The survey equipment was carried noisily and visibly from the van and along the jetty before being placed on deck. The first half of the porcelain, still in the crates marked MACHINE PARTS and CARE, was taken from the shed and stacked in the lowest level of the little boat's hold. There was a strong smell of fish. It was about then that Gallacher started to mutter to himself.

We wrapped the sections of hull in canvas, then I drove the van as far on to the jetty as I dared. We wedged the angular shapes under the bobbing deck.

When the second half of the porcelain and all the other gear had been safely stowed, Hagemann at last came out of the wheelhouse where he'd been listening to Galore. He leaned across me and flipped two switches on the last piece of surveying equipment being slid under cover.

'OK by you, is it, Jimmie?' asked a sweat-covered Gallacher. A startled Hagemann blinked, then nodded. 'Satisfactory,' he said.

I shook my head and lashed down the last corner of tarpaulin.

'All loaded, Captain,' Hagemann told Galore. He turned

away on getting a nod of agreement, tightened a porthole screw, and stepped back into the wheelhouse.

'Crawling git,' I said to Gallacher.

Suddenly it was surprisingly quiet. I could hear the waves lap at the bows of the small boat. I looked round for my loading companion. But Gallacher was on more urgent business. He had taken Romesh by an elbow and was walking him towards the stern. They were both having trouble with their footing.

The Gallacher shoulders were high and stiff. 'I can tell you now, Mr Romesh, I'm not the man for this job! That chanty Hostler said nothing to me down in London about them camera angles o' yours being under the water. Not a bloody word! And that's a fact.' The wind carried the rest of his argument away from me.

By the time they came back on the other side of the wheelhouse, the tone had sharpened. 'In a nutshell, Mr Go-bloody-pal, if you can't offer me double London rates, then it's off I go. Back to civilization. Back to dry bloody land. And it's goin' to cost you two days as it is. Like it or no.'

Romesh said something brief and negative.

Archie swore and jumped back on to the jetty. He got his balance back and turned to glare down. Romesh stared him out.

'You're a hard sod, Gopal,' snarled Gallacher. 'I just hope your underwater epic goes right down the drain. That's a joke, you black bastard. From one potential bankrupt to another. From now on you're down to ten men!' He turned and stalked off towards the hotel.

Romesh turned to me. 'What did he mean by "ten men"? We shall be three men.'

'Football,' I told him. 'The national religion.'

He blinked back at me. 'That is illustration, Nigel. Of

"Need to Know" rationale. You have noted that I did not reveal truth on purpose to him.' He tapped the side of his nose. I nodded. It wasn't the time to argue.

He hadn't finished. 'So now we are without camera skills.' He said it in a pleading voice. I wasn't going to volunteer at that point. I felt I'd been preached to yet again.

After some haggling, I agreed with McWilliam the extra cost of garaging the van in his kippering shed.

We had a fast, late lunch, without seeing Gallacher. We set sail.

Against the horizon, the hills of Sutherland became smaller. On the port side, the sea-lochs of Wester Ross slid past, to be replaced by the high edges of the Isle of Skye; then open water and our first sight below the setting sun of the east coast of South Harris.

Galore had left the wheel to Hagemann. He spoke over Romesh's shoulder. 'Another relic of repression, Mr Gopal. Do you see all those rocks there? And the houses scattered like dust among them? Why would crofting men wish to live there now—on the surface of the Moon?'

Nobody answered him.

'It is because they were all frog-marched there by the agents of the English absentee landlords from far more fertile land on the west of the island.'

Galore suddenly pointed ahead of us.

'Soon you will see less populated but fairer country when we are beyond Rodel and Leverburgh. We shall pass Taransay—where the *machair* has a green gloss and the sheep are fat. It is the aftermath of the Clearances, you understand. The great crime of a past century.'

'When was that?' asked Romesh, his feet splayed for balance.

'A few years ago in time, Mr Gopal. A few years ago. But it feels like yesterday to the people of the Long Island.'

The little boat chugged on. Soon Berneray showed to the south of the Sound of Harris. 'The Prince Charles came there, Mr Gopal. You will have read about that. Away from your yellow journalism.'

Romesh grabbed a rail and leaned into the sharp breeze. Then he turned towards me and shouted into the wind, 'You see! Even His Highness had to escape from attentions of Fleet Street by coming here, Nigel! A Royal lesson for you!' He was perfectly serious.

I kicked the black-painted gunwale.

We turned north into the real Atlantic, skirting the western side of Taransay; a twin-peaked island partly hiding the amazing white sands of Luskentyre. We rounded Scarp. Galore returned to the wheelhouse as the houses on the Brenish shore came and went. The *Girl Mairi* began to struggle in the heavier swell, but we were heading for safe harbour round Gallan Head.

Galore appeared again. Romesh was now staying upright by using both hands. He had turned up the collar of his cotton jacket.

Suddenly it came into view. I heard Galore suck in proud air. 'There she is, Mr Gopal. The finest hotel on the Island of Lewis. And with the finest view.'

Romesh nodded happily but kept his double grip on the rail. He narrowed his eyes.

From sea-level, the Loch Roag Arms was even longer and lower than I remembered. The stone blended into the high rocky backdrop. And, best of all, it didn't seem to be bobbing or pitching about. It looked absolutely stationary. I spread my feet wider on the deck.

'I will hand over the wheel again to your Mr Hagemann!' Galore shouted out. 'You will be in safe hands. It is an honour that I am giving him, you understand. He will take us safely alongside at Valtos.'

At that point, I began to hate Hagemann seriously. And

the cap he had produced after breakfast that morning. I suspected he had laid down his pipe for at least three seconds —to bash, bend and buckle his new headgear into a worn and photogenic shape.

Now he steered the boat deftly alongside the steep concrete steps of the small pier.

'Capital!' declared Galore, and threw the thick white rope up at the small boy waiting on land. '*Tha mi gu math*, young Colin Iain!' he called out in reply to the polite, high-pitched question in Gaelic. Then he added, 'And I just hope that you and Grass have been taking good care of that hotel of mine while I've been on the high seas with these good gentlemen!' He scowled theatrically. The young lad giggled back at him.

We had watched all the naval manœuvres.

'It is refreshing to see such newly-acquired skills, Nigel.'

'I'll break out the champagne.'

'You will read video manual. Concentrating on sharp focus. We shall require you to capture Mr Hagemann's actions for showing to pressmen. You should have little trouble. Cameras have been much simplified.'

'That's a relief,' I told him. 'I'd hate to break into Captain Birdseye's duties at the helm.'

CHAPTER 11

From the lounge window, Romesh and I looked out over the blue-green waters of the Kyles of Pabay. Below the rolling clouds in the blue Hebridean sky, the islands hid the small harbour from the Atlantic breakers. The sun came out, went away, and came again—all in five minutes.

'Not bad for the only place there was.'

'Hotel is most satisfactory, Nigel. View of open seas impeded by green and graceful islands. It is possible to speculate most profitably.'

'I thought we were here to . . .?'

'For other persons to speculate. To imagine Gopal survey vessel disappearing from view, bound for distant sea spot apparently looking for oil deposits. Beyond twelve-mile limitation. While in reality we shall shelter with porcelain behind largest nearby island. It will also ensure that I am less sea-sickened.' He paused. 'What is floating shape, exactly?'

Fifty yards from the shore, a hollow rectangular wooden framework bobbed at anchor. A vivid pink float marked one corner. Days before, I had asked the same question.

'It's a cage, according to Galore. A salmon cage—they farm them in the lochs, then flog them off when they've grown up to over-priced eating houses down in London. No real taste to the fish, he says.'

Romesh moved along the full length of the window, craning his neck. 'And you have battened down hatches over porcelain leaving only survey equipment to be spied upon?'

'Aye, aye, Skipper.'

Galore came in, freshly changed into collar and wool tie. In a Harris Tweed jacket, he looked only slightly less wide. 'It is time to give you a formal welcome to the Loch Roag Arms, Mr Gopal. Let me offer you some Island hospitality. It comes in double measures, you realize.' He winked at us and waited.

'He means would we like a whisky,' I side-mouthed to my left.

Romesh blinked. 'Whisky, then. Kindly.'

Galore's face told us he wasn't used to a general reply. 'Which one, Mr Gopal? A malt or one of these inferior blended affairs?'

To his credit, Romesh remembered the name Gallacher had shouted out in the van outside Inverness.

'Glen Fiddick, kindly.'

'A Glenfiddich it is, then.' Galore pushed his shoulders half way through an opening in the wooden wall-panels and shouted out something in Gaelic. Closing the hatch, he came back and pointed his outsized bottom at the fire in front of us.

'But you will both be wanting to get on with this prospecting of yours. Oil, isn't it?' He laughed at Romesh's queasy silence. 'Never worry, Mr Gopal. Your secret is safe in my hands. Just so long as my wee in-shore boat survives these Atlantic rollers out there. And I receive my fee, of course. Did Mr C. and I not talk last week about a deposit?'

Romesh took the hint. He left me and went with our host towards the picture-window. He was properly serious, his hand already in the inside pocket of his safari jacket.

All at once, the lounge door was kicked open by a straggle-haired twenty-year-old in a green apron bearing three gigantic whiskies on a silver tray. I'd forgotten Scottish single measures started big. Galore arrived back first, still pushing money into his jacket. He dealt out the other two cut-glasses, said '*Slainte mhath!*' again, and downed half the malt in one huge gulp. The barman watched us taking our slow sips and lowered his tray.

Galore clapped his helper on the shoulder of the green sweater. 'John Angus here is the best bar-steward in the west, gentlemen. And the best deputy hotel manager too. Indeed, I sometimes wonder if it is all worth the bother of inn-keeping at all. I could be in the South of France, walking like an Englishman on his very own Promenade des Anglais, and just waiting for my remittance. John Angus here could run this place for me on his own. In fact, he tells me that every week, just after I pay him his money. Isn't that so, John Angus?' He dealt out another back-slap.

The barman showed his gap-teeth and giggled. He headed for the door.

His boss was still musing out loud. 'Ah well, they say the grass is always greener . . .' That time we could hear the barman laugh out loud—and bang the silver tray with an open hand as he left us. I noticed for the first time that, under the green apron, he had on green corduroy trousers.

Galore turned back, the joke, whatever it was, had been a private, Hebridean affair.

'And a great man for appearances,' said our host, taking his second slug of whisky. 'Clean glasses on his shelves, latest cut to his clothes, and a good shine on his bar-counter.'

He stopped. Through the bottom of his glass, he had seen something. 'And talking of appearances, here is our resident dance troupe to entertain you.' He nodded across the wide room. 'Fred and Ginger have arrived. We can all think about having our dinner on time now.'

Through the double doors walked two white-haired men, deep in talk. They both wore green tweed suits and toted well-used fishing gear under arm and over shoulder. Neither of them took any notice of us.

I caught some familiar words I had heard before from my own father: 'Grilse . . . line snap . . . gaff slipping . . . the forecast.'

They stopped to lay down their bags and stack their rods.

'Why "Fred and Ginger", kindly?'

'Two former men of finance, Mr Gopal. Pillars of the Stornoway community. Both retired as bank managers. Which was very bad news for the Atlantic salmon, I can tell you.' Galore left his empty whisky glass on the high mantelshelf. 'People say they talk only of the fishing when they are off the loch and only of banking when they are on it.'

'How do they balance on narrow wooden walkways?'

I saw it first. 'Mr Gopal means, Do they ever make up

their day's catch by dangling a line into a salmon cage?' I forced a weak smile to show that I at least was with him.

Galore turned back to my boss. 'Very good, Mr Gopal! Very good!' He became suddenly serious. 'But I can tell you they would rather cut off their right arm. Or sell their best reel.'

Romesh managed to look both chastened and dogged.

'But why "Fred and Ginger", Mr Macleod?'

'Ah! To fully comprehend that, Mr Gopal, you would have to see these two senior citizens leaping ahead of you for two miles across the heather tussocks towards their fishing loch. Busby Berkeley of Hollywood, USA, could hardly keep up with their choreography.'

We watched the two old boys going up the stairs. They looked deep in thoughts of the next day.

Galore went off, leaving us to admire the weathered décor of a fishing hotel.

Above the dark wooden wall-panels, the cream-plastered walls wore numerous sets of antlers. The only other decoration was a surprised-looking Victorian salmon in a glass case.

Romesh bent to sniff the sweet smell of burning peat. He prodded a slab and jumped back as it exploded under his toe into a powdery cloud. We both drained our glasses.

Beyond the archway leading to the dining-room, a tall, thin man stood for several minutes, looking in. Suddenly, without a word, he was gone, pushing the front door aside with one patched elbow of his Barbour. As we turned to watch his progress outside, Galore came back.

'Who was that, kindly?' Romesh asked.

The face stayed serious. 'Not a person particularly welcome in this hotel—I can tell you that, Mr Gopal. A reporter, he calls himself. From the town. The *Stornoway Free Press*. His is not a column I particularly enjoy. Full of innuendo and hurt. Picked up a lot of other mainland habits in his time away. I would watch what you say to that one, gentlemen.'

The reporter climbed into a beaten-up Volvo with an ancient registration plate. It took him several minutes to point his machine in the right direction. I suddenly realized that the car could have been swung round without any painful reversings towards our boat.

'Just so long as his back wheels don't smash in the top of our hold, wouldn't you say?' I told Romesh.

'Exactly so.' He said it solemnly. He had got the message.

That evening we came down the squeaking, wooden stairs together. I went over to the large map of Lewis and Harris and tried to re-trace our sea-route. I began to have trouble with the back-breaking Gaelic place-names.

Romesh had fiddled with the fishing scales and was reading the menu pinned to the doorpost when Galore came along the corridor. 'We are looking forward to your tales of civilization, gentlemen. Come away through and I will let Grass ease your throats beforehand.' We walked after him and ducked our heads.

The small bar lay at the end of the hallway. Behind the Formica top stood the same young barman we had seen before. He wore a different top-half—a green, matching, corduroy shirt. The collar had green buttons holding the tips down. I now realized what Galore's in-joke in the lounge had been about.

From side-on, he had an Adam's apple as large as one of his Optic measures. His oversized head was framed by an amazing spread of whisky bottles. There were no other spirit bottles to be seen.

'John Angus, look after our guests. See that they do not drop from thirst a second time.'

The barman nodded first at Romesh.

'I am awaiting Mr Grass, thank you.'

I had to hiss my message fast. 'That's him! They don't use the nicknames to their faces!'

Romesh was still blinking.

'Glen Fiddick, kindly, Mr Angus,' he said at last. Someone sniggered at a back table. At the far end of the bar which looked out over the mirror-flat waters of the Kyles, stood two local teenagers. I recognized the twang of their Lewis Gaelic. The one word I could make out was 'oil'.

Grass served us quickly. With a polite nod, he went back to talk to his cronies. I caught that one English word a second time.

By our next round, the barman had decided it was time for the local niceties. The ones I had gone through from Galore on my first trip. Grass asked us when we had arrived. And when we would be leaving. Then he waited, hand on chin, for Romesh to tell him everything about his life to date.

After another half-hour, Hagemann came into the bar, looked towards us and left. He was heading pointedly for the dining-room.

The meal was Scotch broth, followed by sea trout smothered in oatmeal. Hagemann managed to stay half a course ahead of Romesh and me. At the end, he excused himself through teeth clamped to pipe-stem. I thought I heard something about an early, sober start and burped into my napkin.

Back in the bar again, Romesh picked up on the story of his earlier commercial career in Uganda. Grass threw in some finely-timed 'Well, well's'. I concentrated on my whisky.

My boss changed to his current favourite—the supply of London property sites. The barman heard him out, then giggled over his polishing cloth. 'You know, sir, you are reminding me of the other Londoners we get coming in. They are fond of talk of fine premises too, just like yourself.'

Romesh lifted an eyebrow.

'Hyde Park, Mayfair, Piccadilly. We even christened the older one of them "St James", did we not, Murdoch?' One of Grass's mates from the far end raised his beer-glass in agreement. 'Oh, aye,' he chortled. 'Very genteel.'

'They were fond of their dram too,' Grass told us. 'As fond of the whisky as they were of their London whelks and winkles.'

I stopped in mid-drink.

'And they were great men for the hospitality, were they not, Murdoch?'

This time, the young drinker said something which sounded like 'Ha' from the far end. Then he nodded his head too much. He had been at the bar for the whole time we had been eating dinner.

'You mean they fell over after a couple of stiff ones,' I said, to cover up what I had really noticed.

'I mean, sir, that you could catch them drinking in here on many a night. And you could have a good crack with them too. They would even buy a round—from time to time. But there was no real give-and-take, gentlemen. That is what we all noticed here in the Loch Roag. There was never an invitation up to their White Lodge. Not for any local man, anyway.'

He moved away to serve Fred, who had just come in. Or it could have been Ginger.

Romesh pressed on with the Glenfiddich. By the end of the night, Grass's drinking friend had come along the counter and bought us doubles. He then pulled the plug on the Country & Western burbling out of the jukebox in the back corner and treated the whole bar to a live Gaelic song. At last I led my employer away by his less-bent elbow.

On the landing outside our bedrooms, Romesh paused

unsteadily, both hands on the balustrade, as if he was still at sea.

'I am looking forward to sound night's sleep, Nigel. Tomorrow it is important that we first make urgent preparations. Mention of Busby Berkeley has given me thought. We too shall mount big production. I must discuss fine points with Dr Hagemann at first light. With you also.' I didn't, at that point, notice the promotion of my team-mate.

He made a first, unsuccessful, pass at his doorknob. 'These innocent island people are most refreshing, Nigel. I feel rekindled.'

'It's the firewater, Romesh.' I turned back towards him. 'I'm not so happy about some of their old drinking pals. Posh Londoners wolfing down winkles and whelks? And what about that journalist we saw buzz our boat? Didn't expect a snooper on Day One.'

Romesh thought. 'He is not a friend of Mr Galore.'

'Who do you reckon passed on the info about us, then?'

'What is cost of telephone call from Ullapool to Stornoway?'

'Eh?'

'McWilliam. You've forgotten, Nigel. Alexander Graham Bell was Scotsman. Good night.'

The floor of the bare bedroom creaked again. I forced the bedclothes apart and fell into the crisp sheets. Through the thin wall, I could hear the heavy breathing as he pulled his clothes off. Suddenly there was the sound of something heavy being dragged across the linoleum. And Romesh scraping metal against metal. I had forgotten about the padlocked bag. I couldn't remember seeing it on the boat.

CHAPTER 12

My head ached and my throat hurt. In the bathroom mirror the whites of my eyes looked as if a mad pavement artist had gone over them with a thin red pen. I did the usual first-morning-thing and checked my hairline for the onset of baldness. Which meant touching my temples. They were red-hot. I promised myself to reduce the intake of malt whisky.

The tap-water jumped out of my cupped hands and threw soapy foam into my face. I had forgotten the incredible softness of the water on the island. The bubbles were bursting too noisily for me.

All at once I heard mice. In my bedroom. Singing, Gaelic mice. Levering my dripping upper-half round the doorpost, I found myself staring at a neat, rounded, black-skirted Hebridean bottom. The song sounded sad but sweet.

She must have felt my eyes on her; she straightened up quickly from the folded bedclothes, laughed, and said something I couldn't make out. It sounded cheerful.

'Didn't catch that. No speaka da lingo, I'm afraid, Lovely.'

With an effort, she turned up the volume to the barely audible. 'I was wishing you a good morning, Mr Carlton. In English.' Another gurgle from behind the delicate white hand to tiny un-made-up face. Her skin was amazing.

I told her to keep up the good work, just caught the first two names she whispered at me, and went back to the soapsuds.

By the time I came back, she had gone.

It was as I pulled on the Aran pullover that I realized that there had been no sounds of any sort from next door.

No heavy bare feet, no shoes, no slippery bars of soap, no Hindu moans, no bangs. Not even soft female crooning. Nothing. I opened my door gently and crept along the short corridor.

'What was laughter, kindly?'

His face was almost as white as mine had been in the mirror. Which meant he felt even worse. His head was staying where it was, embedded in the pillow. Only the eyes and lips moved.

'Just the maid. Making up.' I paused for effect and won a pained frown.

'The bed, Romesh. Nice girl, but giggly. Wouldn't let it worry you.'

His forehead didn't uncrease. 'We must remain pure. Remember Cæsar's wife.'

'You'll have to tell me. Kampala High was obviously ahead of my prep school.'

'It is William Shakespeare, Nigel. And I am really talking to you of women in general.'

I could see the bump in the scrambled bedclothes where his toes were showing his displeasure. 'I am thinking of ultimate success of expedition. You do not see Mr Hagemann running after—'

'Perhaps if you were to pull yourself upright, you might just—'

'You are being flippant once more!' he growled, and hauled himself on to one elbow. 'I was merely giving you literary allusion to prove need for protection of collective reputation. We must cultivate image. As dedicated scientists.'

It all seemed one of his ruses. To distract me. 'Are you going to get up today?' I asked.

'Sir Churchill used bed for maximum creativity. This morning I have decided to devote to major planning. We are in need of over-view for next three critical days. I shall emerge with same at noon.'

'You mean you're *not* going to get up?'

He was now clutching the top edge of the sheet defensively. I carried on the attack. 'I'll tell Mary Flora not to tuck you in, in that case.'

The heavy brow furrowed again.

'The maid. The one you don't want me to sexually harass.'

I looked at my watch. 'Three hours will just give Herr Kapitän Hagemann and me time to get on with the more boring nautical tasks.' Then I remembered something said the night before. 'Or should I say "Herr Doktor"?'

'Mr Hagemann has already been instructed,' he told me. 'Last evening, before meal, we discussed together technical details of survey equipment. He is fully aware of just what to do this morning.'

'So why the Doctor bit?'

'It is for effect. Oil companies employ scientific seekers. We must appear to be oil company for present.'

'So why not "Doctor Carlton", may I ask, Doctor Gopal?'

That didn't please him either. 'It is question of credibility, Nigel.' He grasped more blanket. 'But if it annoys you, I shall only address him so in conversation with outside parties.'

'Right.' I felt my mouth loosen slightly. 'That's the intellectual bit sewn up. And the technological side. Just leaves swabbing down the decks for you to delegate, I reckon. I'll see you over the top of my bucket at high noon then.'

My sarcasm was wasted.

'By that time, I shall have prepared detailed documentary analysis.' It sounded pompous to me.

I looked at my watch again.

'Just missed out on breakfast, worrying about your physical condition. Bet you the Kapitän's down there with his manual propped up against his bowl of porridge. Couldn't face food myself, somehow. Not with this head.'

He looked pathetic, lying there. For no good reason, I weakened.

'I'll get them to send up some Alka-Seltzer, if it's going to get you out of your mood.'

'I am quite in order, thank you kindly.'

With an agonized face, he suddenly threw his cotton-striped top-half forward and down and stretched across the floor to where he had dropped his work sheets. The effort to get horizontal again without help from me was painful to watch.

'I'd better be off then. Hate to hold up any totally deep thinking.'

'Be prepared for action by midday at latest!' he shouted at my back.

'I'll warn Captain Birdseye. Tell him to get his oiling and greasing out of the way well before then.'

'You must treat with respect, Nigel! We are dependent on specialist skills, remember!' He started to wrestle with the giant bits of paper.

I slammed the door and headed for the stairs.

Instead of having breakfast, I decided on a slice of dry toast from the serving table. I walked it into the empty lounge, away from the deafening noises of other people's coffee- and tea-drinking and marmalade crashing against buttered, floury baps.

I walked past the ash-strewn fireplace, looked out through the picture window, and saw what I'd been afraid of. Hagemann was bustling about the *Girl Mairi*. Even at a distance, he looked appallingly fit and photogenic. I winced and flopped on to the sofa.

Picking up a glossy from the coffee table, I bit into the toast. But it wasn't a magazine, it was an art-house catalogue. I looked again at the cover. Some newsagent had written 'White Lodge, Valtos' in the top corner. I looked inside. Under each coloured photograph, prices had been scrawled. Big 'hammer' prices. Every one had a 'K' in front. The dealer's estimates were also in thousands. It had been quite a sale.

My bent head began to throb again. I went outside and gulped Hebridean fresh air. The time had come to do something.

In the hundred yards to the tiny quay, the weather changed three times. Clouds scudded from horizon to horizon, rain spat for one minute—and just as suddenly stopped. A skittish breeze rose, worried at my hair, then disappeared. It was a typical Lewis day.

On the boat, Hagemann did say, 'Good morning.' Through the stem of his pipe and clenched Robert Taylor teeth.

'I'm well ahead, Carlton,' he added. 'Just one or two very simple, technical bits and bobs to finish off.'

He looked me up and down as if the bits and bobs were beyond me. He was keeping his body in the doorway of the wheelhouse, guarding the survey gear from marauders.

I told him the thing I would be doing, then went and started to do it. It was the best way to cure my sore head and not punch him.

Ten minutes later, Hagemann stuck his head out of the doorway again. 'Short trip!' he shouted. 'Don't worry, we'll barely touch the Atlantic! Giving the engine a test! Don't let me stop you swabbing that deck!' I didn't respond.

Looking up from my mop for the first time, feet wide apart on the deck, I gazed back towards the shore. The hotel had gone behind the little island Galore had called Vacsay. I could still see the steep hill which lay at the back of the Loch Roag. The sky had now filled with steel-grey clouds. All at once a shaft of sunlight broke through and skipped across the barren landscape, hitting every rock. And, even more quickly, it lit up a long, single-storeyed wooden building I hadn't noticed until then. Now it shone out from the hillside as starkly as a wolf's fang. It had to be the White Lodge.

The blue shutters across each window emphasized the newly-painted white planking. One shutter banged in the warm wind. There was no real reason for it, but I shivered.

The sudden sun lasted only seconds before the clouds regrouped. I saw for the first time the single clump of trees in the dead ground between the two buildings which had made the Lodge invisible from the hotel below.

Thirty rolling and pitching minutes later, my job of swabbing down almost over and Hagemann looking as self-satisfied as ever, we edged alongside the little Valtos quay.

One person had come to meet us. The locked leather bag was at his ankle, the flapping sheets of large paper under one arm.

'Ah! The tablets of stone,' I told him, looking at the Critical Path sheets.

'Explain, kindly.'

'Just a literary allusion. See you got up, after all.'

Irritated, Romesh shifted the work sheets to beneath his other elbow and looked pointedly over my shoulder.

'It is all looking very good. Shipshape and Plymouth-fashion. It will photograph very well. Ready for big day.' Just to annoy me, he was talking exclusively to Hagemann.

'How's the head now, Romesh?' I asked, loudly.

'Side-scan sonar is functional, Mr Hagemann?'

He told him Yes, Mr Gopal. Mr Gopal unfolded the first double sheet and ticked off an entry.

'Navigation equipment also, Doctor . . .?' He looked rapidly at me before correcting himself. 'Mister Hagemann?'

He told him Yes, Mr Gopal. Mr Gopal ticked that one off too.

Then he whispered. 'What is position with pre-prepared read-out, Mr Hagemann? It has survived journey northwards intact?'

His intellectual equal told him, It is ready for presentation to the local press, yes, Mr Gopal. I thought for a moment Hagemann was going to touch the peak of the cap but he restrained himself.

Another big, obvious tick on the work sheets. Smirks all round. Romesh beamed at his star employee. He looked down at the deck at a lurid plastic pile.

'What are these, kindly?'

'Marker buoys. Bought them from a local lobster-fisherman. They will demarcate our search positions. Visible for miles.' His teeth readjusted themselves on his pipe-stem.

Someone liked it. 'First class. First class.'

And he didn't even ask Hagemann how much they had cost, as he would have done with me. And it was even given a fresh line on the Gopal Critical Path sheets.

He was now looking towards Vacsay. 'Can I be sure boat is invisible from shore when behind small island?'

'We will be completely unseen, Mr Gopal.'

'Exactly so.'

So that was the real reason for our trip round the bay. I felt excluded. And hurt. I had checked out the position of the island, as requested, on my first trip to the place.

'Haven't been completely idle myself this morning, Mr Gopal. Sir.' I shouldered the mop.

But he had already turned, back towards his pet. He almost put an arm round a shoulder. I heard the beginning. 'Mr Hagemann, tell kindly. There are certain jargon phrases I should use when dealing with journalists at later date. Such as sediments . . . You have additional suggestions?'

I just caught the start of the Hagemann waffle as they left me and began to walk round the small craft.

After that there was only the lapping of water against the hull and the irritated swishing of my mop. Then gradually louder words. They were coming back from their cosy seaside chat.

'Exactly so,' Romesh was cooing. He looked up and saw me for what looked like the first time.

His face lost the smug look. It hardened. 'What is position with non-technical aspects, Nigel?' I noticed that his pencil was poised over the lower half of the work sheet, below the thick red line.

'A doddle, really,' I heard myself say. 'First of all I checked out the non-technical porcelain. You know, the stuff we're up here to work on. Still safely below decks and under lock and key.' I looked at a broken finger-nail.

'That is good, Nigel.' The tick seemed reluctant.

'Then I ran my eye over the non-technical scuba gear. You know, the stuff that'll get us down there and safely up again.'

I waited until the pencil was about to hit the paper. 'One small problem, maybe. No sign of either oxygen cylinder. Reckon Gallacher could have half-inched them while we were eating? In lieu of wages?' The pencil hovered. 'I leave you to seek out replacements, Nigel.'

'He's the one who really needs one, Romesh!' I jabbed my head towards Hagemann. 'I'm just the slob behind the underwater camera!'

'You are in charge of stocks, Nigel. You are warehouse-man.'

He made a rapid note in my colour of ink against the entry on his sheet.

I hadn't managed to derail him. In fact, things had got rapidly worse.

'You have accounted for scaffolding poles for survey readings?'

'My next job. After I finish the demanding task of swabbing down the decks. More nautical square feet than I reckoned.'

'Very well, Nigel,' but the tone of voice indicated the opposite. 'While you are completing delayed forenoon duties, I can complete discussion of survey aspects of shooting script for next three days with Mr Hagemann. Since he is fully up to date with current tasks.' That was bitchy.

'I'll think through how to dump our fragile stuff safely on the sea-bed while I'm scrubbing away, Romesh.'

He scowled. 'Nigel, it is time for you to realize. We are here in this wild place to be showmen, not artisans. Remember we are oil-men who by chance will find sunken Dutch sailing vessel bearing great treasure. It is initial display of survey skills which will guarantee success of expedition. Big production for next days. It is media we shall seek to impress and deceive. We must leave you to handle logistics of china-dropping.'

'Right then, Romesh. Before the elephants get into the ring, this particular clown had better get on with the dull bits. Single-handed, it would appear.' I hadn't liked his collective, Hagemann-embracing pronoun.

'You will be assisted by diving team,' he told me.

'They don't look all that useful, actually.'

He frowned at me, then hurriedly peered at the second page of the work sheets. He read it out slowly, as if dealing with a ten-year-old. 'Divers arrive in Stornoway Monday on ferry-boat from mainland. Then by Dormobile across island to this place.' He looked up for confirmation.

'So who,' I demanded, 'are those dusky gents wandering about the foreshore in scuba masks and webbed feet?' With some satisfaction, I pointed over his podgy shoulder towards the wide strand of white sand beyond the quay. He swung round. It was high time he suffered.

CHAPTER 13

'Our complete plans will be awry!' Romesh spluttered it out as he galloped up the steep path to the hotel, work sheets under arm, me in pursuit.

'They've got to be our boys,' I gasped. 'An advance party from London. Sharmila's probably sent them on ahead to acclimatize.'

'They are speaking Urdu! It is not Bengali!' He didn't turn round to snap that out.

Romesh shouldered the doors apart and marched towards the telephone in the lobby. As his finger made its last digital swirl, I saw the outline of Galore in the opaque glass of the door leading to the offices. He was coming towards us. I jabbed my finger towards what would be a cheaper source of information on our mystery deep-sea divers. 'It'll save you the cost of a long-distance,' I told my boss.

'Who are those people, kindly? Webfooted people?' Romesh was asking the question even before the door closed behind Galore.

Galore's stride pattern didn't change. He had been ambling towards his own front door anyway. He looked through the glass, then turned, just as slowly.

'Don't you worry about them, Mr Gopal. Young Mohammed and his brother wouldn't hurt a fly. They might dissect a mollusc, mind you. Marine biology is their game. Every Wednesday. It is the half-day, you understand.'

He did not get understood. 'You have Moslem business persons in Valtos?' Romesh's face was an interesting mix.

'In Stornoway, Mr Gopal. It is the half-day there.' He kept his own face straight, but only just. 'I should tell you that their family has been in Lewis for over thirty years. Almost a clan, some people would tell you.' He swung round to head back towards his accounts. 'Buying up the shops at a great rate. Some of them have even taken up the Gaelic, they are such traders. And with a very good line in fitted carpets.' The glass door swung shut.

Romesh looked down at the receiver in his right hand and banged it back into its cradle. 'Why do they allow such immigrants?' he demanded.

He then did what he often does after a panic. 'We must let nothing shake mental resolve, Nigel. We must condition our minds for next two days. This is Big Production. Here is what we must do . . .'

'Dr Hagemann,' he rumbled, across the table—just loudly enough to be overheard, 'I think today we are entirely fatigued. So many negative soundings. So much sediment on sea-bed. Do you think there is purpose in going onwards in such barren place? Pass sprouts, kindly.'

I kept my head down, eating while Hagemann did the 'There, there. Come, come,' bit, as he had been told to.

Almost before he had finished, Romesh was into his second stage-whisper. 'Still, I feel in heart of hearts that at last we must strike lucky! These charts which you were fortunate enough to locate in depths of National Maritime Museum library must be believed. No matter how ancient and stained in sea-water. I feel it in my bones. No matter how exhausted we are. Courage, my friend!' He wiped a crumb of oatcake from his mouth. 'You also, Mr Carlton.'

'What the hell are you saying, Romesh!' I whispered it. Really whispered, I mean. So as not to be overheard.

He had his bland look on, but at least he lowered his own voice. 'Second part of deception, Nigel. We have moved on.'

Out of the side of my vision I thought I saw Hagemann smirk.

My mouth stopped chewing and stayed open.

Romesh pressed on, bent forward. 'We must now become treasure-seekers. It is just before we locate sensational artefacts.'

As I tried to take in the change in our script, I could see the other diners lean back to rest their ears.

I cleared my throat and said loudly, 'I definitely think we should make one last boat-run at it, sir. We'll strike oil tomorrow morning, you'll see!' I could tell from Romesh's expression that I was behind in the game. Not to mention overplaying. The rest of the dinner passed in silence.

The next morning, Friday, we took another seemingly-furtive trip from the quay—once we had got an audience. But now there was much swinging of lead weights, a first unwrapping of the metal-seeking magnetometer, and staring at ancient sea charts. I remembered to trip over one of the bright orange marker buoys around as we set out. Romesh clattered several scaffolding poles together as Hagemann took the boat out of the tiny Valtos harbour and pointed her towards open sea. That day was our day for going north. Uselessly north. The Romesh script told us it was the last day on which we would find nothing. Noisily.

Saturday was different again. With the same sly-looking preparations for departure and the shaking out of old navigational paper, we steered ourselves south. Towards what Romesh shouted out was his St Kilda Gap. The two-mile stretch of open water, carefully beyond the twelve-mile limit.

All of which nautical movement was imaginary. Once the *Girl Mairi* had jogged round the first small island and got out of sight of the spectators in front of the Loch Roag Arms, we pitched and tossed at anchor for four boring hours until

Romesh ordered us off again, back to our warm Valtos home.

'At last, Nigel. We are about to escape from inhibitions of pretence. From tomorrow everything can be open and above.' He was clutching the rope stay for support, his feet wide apart.

'Do we play at keeping the treasure-spot under wraps, Romesh? In your magic St Kilda Gap?'

'Exactly so.'

'What if some boat follows . . .?'

He really gritted his teeth. 'They will think that we are masters of subterfuge, Nigel! Laying false trail. But only if we keep up such aura of mystery at all times. It will call for heavy play-acting by us all. At mealtimes especially.'

It was a heavy hint, I thought. 'Next meal, I'll do a Hertz —try harder. Just that I was really hungry that night. More verbal skills over the lentil soup, right?'

There was no head movement. 'Merely take lead from Mr Hagemann, Nigel.'

'My thought entirely.' I wasn't finding it easy to hide that I was hurt. 'What do you need me to do? Look after the cracked plates? That bag at your ankle?'

'It will be quite enough for you to verify that video equipment is fully functional,' he told me. 'I shall require from you first-class close-ups of Mr Hagemann locating treasure for first time.'

That didn't help. 'Pity he isn't going to be able to suck on it. Underwater.'

He stared.

'His pipe.'

He turned away from me. We had reached the friendly little Valtos quay.

That Saturday evening, our dinner-table chat was even louder. Earlier, in the bar, Romesh had started to wave the

faked print-outs from the side-scan sonar he and Hagemann
had concocted in Beckenham.

Our landlord—and Grass—began to rub their eyes at
that point. And Fred and Ginger stopped talking about
their day's catch when Romesh unravelled his largest, most
exciting graph. His stage-whisper as he pushed it back into
his inside pocket was beautifully timed.

'You are quite sure, Dr Hagemann? It is entirely outside
limitation? And shadow outline is definitely of ancient mer-
chantman? But how can you tell me it is positively Dutch
by looking at silhouette only?'

Hagemann leaned forward and muttered 'Abracadabra,'
under his breath, exactly as he had been ordered.

'Exactly so!' Romesh wheezed loudly. 'Most satisfactory!'

In spite of what I'd promised earlier, I concentrated
on the Caboc cream cheese. Slicing through the oatmeal
coating, I left it to the two stars to glitter conversationally.

It was now Sunday. Day of rest. There was a lot we had to
do.

There was now more real work to get through than we'd
carried out in our entire stay on the island. And it was all
to take place in twelve feet of photogenic water. Just deep
enough to make it look as if we were several hundred feet
down and twelve and one-half miles out from the Isle of
Lewis.

As we chugged round the rocks at the near-end of Vacsay,
I looked back as usual to check that we were not being
followed. The quay itself was empty and the boats of the
lobster-fishermen bobbed idly on the water. There was not
one newly-scrubbed morning face to be seen at the big
window of the Loch Roag Arms.

Romesh had picked out the Presbyterian Sabbath for our
hyper-activity with good reason. The only sound I could
pick up over the putter-putter of our engine was the dry

rattle of that shutter on the White Lodge, high above the hotel. It kept on, setting my teeth on edge. And in front of the low, locked building, another gleam of sunlight hit the chrome of a radiator grille under some tarpaulin sheeting.

Suddenly one baleful bell began to ring out. And two hundred yards further along, down towards the shore, beyond the white strip of wind-bleached sand, the first worshippers walked into our view. Stick-like L. S. Lowry creatures, but moving. Moving past the drystone wall of the burial-ground towards the church on the bare edge of the other hill behind the hotel. No one in Valtos would be interested in three foreigners breaking their Sabbath.

The boat was now motionless behind our little island. At last I got to unlock the hatches. Moving as fast and as silently as we could, the three of us began to pile up the mounds of fragile porcelain on the strip of deck on each side of the hold.

Then it was my job to unravel the prefabricated sections of hull. They would be lowered to the sea-bed first, as a necessary photographic backdrop to the real Chinese treasure.

I was handed out the boring job of filling the baskets, while our employer played with the boat's hoist.

Hagemann had accepted the task of lowering the pieces into their final, sandy, position.

Stripping down to his designer shorts, the first thing he did was to turn down my offer of flippers and mask. Instead, he bared his heatlamp-bronze chest, waggled muscular legs over the edge of the diving grating we had lowered over the side of the boat, and slipped down into the water with the first loaded basket.

Putting the last empty basket to one side, I was leaning over the rail helping Romesh up from the diving platform when I heard the slight noise from sea-ward. I sprinted into the wheelhouse, stubbed my toe on the locked bag which Romesh had quietly stowed there, and grabbed the binoculars. I pointed them at the rocks.

High above the shoreline, slipping and slithering away from us, I saw the tweedy backs of our old fishermen.

'Romesh! We've been spotted! Over there, on your titchy bloody island! The one that was supposed to hide everything!'

The glasses were grabbed from me, the lanyard still tight around my neck.

He peered towards Vacsay.

'It is awful Fred and awful Ginger! Confound all flying fishermen! Why should they choose to do this today? Is nothing sacred—even in North of Scotland?'

He let the heavy glasses go. They swung back and thumped me on the chest. I said nothing. While Romesh had been panicking, I could hear the faint scraping of ancient feet as they scrambled up the rocks above the water's edge. For oldies, they moved at amazing speed.

'It is no use, Nigel. We will have to buy silence.'

'You really think they saw exactly what we were doing? I'm sure that last basket of stuff was already out of—'

'I shall offer them one thousand pounds each as price.'

'Romesh, you're talking about bribing two retired Scottish bank managers!'

'Two thousand pounds to each person, then. That is maximum amount possible.'

He had misunderstood me again.

The journey back to the quay should have been light-hearted and free from stress. Instead it was tense. Romesh stood with one foot on the bow-rail, already poised to jump on to dry land. There was someone waiting for him.

'Fred and Ginger would very much like to have a wee

word with you about your trip, Mr Gopal.' Galore, for once, looked serious.

Romesh took one step back before his feet hit the coiled rope on the deck.

CHAPTER 14

Romesh started to talk rapidly. 'I wish to offer you . . .'

I noticed that neither of them had their hands out to take money.

It was Fred who spoke for them. 'We would like to think, Mr Gopal, that you did not see exactly what we were doing. Over on yon wee island.'

'Exactly so.' I had never heard him say it with such doubt. There was not a glimmer of a head movement.

Ginger had a voice like his thick white hair. 'In fact, Mr Gopal, Mr Carlton, it would be better if you were to say that you did not see us outside of the hotel at all.'

'Exactly so.' I didn't mean it as a joke. It just came out.

Fred chimed in again. 'You see, gentlemen, we are both of us, you understand, highly thought of in this community. People look up to us every day of the week. Every day.' As he talked, Fred's lined hands were worrying away at the green tweed knees of his plus-fours.

'Exactly so.' We actually said it to them together. Without looking at one another.

'Then that is capital, just capital, Mr Gopal!' Fred's hands stopped working at the tweed. He stood up, relief written all over his weather-beaten face.

His friend still had something to say to me. He whispered it. 'Could you two gentlemen be doing with a bit of a fish to be taking away with you, Mr Carlton? I dare say if our friend Galore was to look in his deep freeze, he could lay a hand on a catch of ours. From last week it would be, of course.' Then he winked.

We tottered out of the stuffy room. Romesh was too busy wiping sweat away to talk.

I filled in the gap. 'Didn't understand too much of all that. Somehow they were more scared about something than we were. What do you think? Gun-running? Drugs?'

'Exactly so,' he mumbled, eyes still glazed.

This time we walked rather than ran along the lobby. Later, I was to kick myself for not noticing then that the only items against the dark, panelled walls were our own props—a magnetometer in a canvas wrapping, flippers and masks, weighted diving belts, some grappling hooks and clamps, a couple of rubber-clad compasses. All to give the latest message about our real reason for being there.

Heading towards the breakfast-room that next morning, we passed the office. Galore looked up from his room-occupancy chart.

'I don't know what reassurance you offered these old boys, Mr Gopal, but whatever way you put it, the two of them fairly danced towards their dinner table last night. And they were still buying each other drams an hour after you all bade us an early good night! Is it not wonderful what a clear conscience will do for banking men? They had quite convinced themselves you were heading straight up that hill to inform the minister himself.'

'The Minister?' Romesh beat me to it. I was still trying to choose between Defence and the Home Office.

'The Reverend Timothy Murdo I am talking of. Stalwart of the Lord's Day Observance Society. Scourge of all Sabbath-breathers.'

Romesh beat me again. 'You are implying, Mr Macleod, that ancient fishing men had religious reasons to fear having been seen from our Sunday pleasure cruise?'

'Have you ever seen my front hallway bare of their rods and reels and them inside the place on any other day of the week?'

We both shook our heads. It was what I had missed as we had come through the lobby.

'And *I* have never seen two old rogues running into my hotel so rapidly to put their feet up on my best coffee table and pretend to be taking an afternoon nap. It was only the four feet being in wellingtons that gave their game away. That and them nudging each other when our wee boat hove into view.'

Romesh had fastened on to one word. 'What game, kindly?'

'Why, casting two illicit Sunday fishing lines into a sea-loch! In full view, they had to tell me, of you and your men, Mr Gopal! You were innocent bystanders to a crime worse than murder by the lights of the Rev. Timothy Murdo. A weekday murder, at any rate.'

'So they are now much relieved?' Romesh was looking much relieved too—visibly recoiling from his Monday-morning wobblies.

'They now think of you and your young companions as gentlemen beyond reproach. Proper diplomats. Such discretion, they were saying last night.'

There was something behind Galore's twinkling eyes I couldn't make out. 'And what's your own opinion, Mr Macleod?'

'The very same, Mr Carlton. Backed up by the evidence of my own eyes and ears. I would agree indeed that I have never had a trio of guests with such finesse—in so many directions. Not only do you reassure two fine old fishermen who fancied a trawl of Vacsay on the Sabbath, but you were able for three whole days to lull the rest of us in this hotel into thinking you were seekers after oil-bearing strata. And that takes some doing.' The eyes were glinting at me again. 'While all that time you were chasing something altogether more exotic.'

He stood the room-occupancy sheets on end and knocked their edges square. 'We do not look askance at a bit of skilful subterfuge on this island, however. And don't you worry, the two of you. As with Fred and Ginger, your secret is safe in my keeping.' He paused. 'Just so long, mind, as the press reports make passing mention of the one good hotel on the west side of Lewis. I wish you a hearty breakfast, gentlemen.'

Galore turned back to his charts. 'Now, about that room I was chasing up for a Miss Gopal . . .'

We walked on.

'Fred and Ginger really didn't see it! They'd have blackmailed us if they had!' I hissed. 'But what about Galore? You'd think *he* was the one who'd been watching us do the drop!'

He looked thoughtful. 'Exactly so.' But that was all.

It was probably the sight of someone else's work sheets that did it. Even before I had plunked for porridge instead of Weetabix, Romesh was into an inside pocket and unfurling his own sheets of paper. He barely nodded at Hagemann's arrival at table. The waitress, instead of an order for breakfast, was asked a question from line six, page two of his Critical Path sheets.

'When does morning ship arrive at Stornoway from Ullapool, kindly?'

Her reply was the usual soft Gaelic-accented whisper.

'Once again, if you please, young lady?'

She increased the volume after a shy giggle towards me and told Romesh the boat would arrive around 10.0 a.m.

'And road journey from port of Stornoway to Valtos is how long?'

'I can tell you all that, Romesh!' I interrupted, annoyed

at his lousy memory. 'Who do you think was your advance party?'

Romesh smiled up at the waitress and told her, 'Egg as usual, kindly.' She headed off towards the kitchen.

'It'll take Sharmila and the divers a couple of hours. Maybe more,' I added. Another meal had been spoiled.

Romesh took my pen from me. I watched him write 'Noon' in the relative space. Then he looked overleaf, back to page one, and found the unfilled slot.

'You have not yet told result of checking video equipment for morning's first filming, Nigel.'

My teeth missed the edge of the piece of toast.

Still wiping my mouth, I hared up the shorter back stairs to my bedroom – to where the small black cases lay piled.

Checking the working of the TV monitor was simple. Then I ticked off the underwater lights and the spare bulb supply, the extension leads and plugs, the batteries. They were all there. The camera sat in its polystyrene bed. Something made me lift it out, heft it on to my left shoulder, and point it out of the high window under the sloping roof.

At an acute angle, I twirled the ring to focus down on our boat. There, in the viewfinder, was Hagemann—fresh from his breakfast of half an ounce of dry muesli, no added sugar. He was already in the wheelhouse fiddling with that cap and combing his moustache for the forthcoming photo session. I realized for the first time that there was something wrong with the weight of the camera. I flipped open the side hatch. The empty side hatch.

My next movements were a frantic jump across to the box of cassettes and a scrabble to unzip the photo-bag and open up the lid. Of an empty box of cassettes. My kick sent it skittering across the linoleum. I headed for the door, stomach heaving, and took the steps three at a time.

'Romesh! Gallacher! The sod didn't just stop at oxygen

cylinders! Cleaned us out of bloody video tape too! Even the one in the camera!'

He took it relatively calmly. First he held out my pen, now that there was nothing to note on his chart. Then he said, 'You will telephone ahead to Stornoway shop. Hotel will provide urgent transport to drive straight across island. I shall allow total of three hours since you are familiar with whole road. You will start now.'

The next shock was in the kitchens, at Galore's elbow.

'Not today, Mr C. It has already gone. You've picked on the very day our runabout is already in Stornoway. It is struggling to get a test certificate as we are talking to one another.' He clapped my shoulder with a hand like a ton weight. 'You can blame it all on the Minister of Transport and his big-city bureaucracy.'

Romesh was just as decisive that second time. 'You will leave message with steamer people. Sharmila will be instructed to pick up tapes on vay through town.' Only the slipping 'w' gave me any clue to his inner tension.

The rest of that morning was painful. Listening to Romesh explain to him why we couldn't carry out even the first segment of filming—the finding of the treasure of the deep, starring Dr Mervyn Hagemann, scientist. Hagemann sulked.

The sea was getting rougher. The wavelets, even at the quayside, were beginning to take on white caps. And the tethered lobster boats chipped nevously at each other, next to our larger boat.

After two hours, there were no other jobs to spin out our time. All the tackle and gear had been lugged down from the Loch Roag lobby, every moving part on the boat had been oiled and greased at least twice. I walked past the tea-chest and that heavy, locked bag several times.

By having three cups of coffee each, we made the morning break in the hotel lounge last out for forty minutes. It was an improvement on munching sandwiches at anchor out on the Atlantic.

It was still only 11.45. Romesh started to doze. Hagemann marched across and stood at the window, looking hard right —from where he could be first to spot the Dormobile on the ribbon of road leading down into Valtos.

But noon came and there was no prissy shout from across the airless room. A quarter of an hour later Romesh woke up. 'No sign,' I told him. He stared back, eyes unfocused. I got up and walked into the cold lobby and picked up the telephone.

'It will take me a good few minutes, Mr Gopal.' I didn't bother to correct the man. The tone of the voice from MacBrayne's Stornoway harbour office was telling me that confirming a disembarked Miss Gopal and one crowded Dormobile would mean checking a full passenger-list. I waited, getting more anxious as the minutes clicked by on my digital watch.

The relaxed, negative answer made me feel worse. 'So when *will* this second boatload get there?' I shouted down the line. I was told, again too calmly, that it would be at his quayside by 9.0 p.m. Weather permitting. I would have to do something else about six video tapes.

The Stornoway shopowner took it in his stride. 'You can calm down, Mr Carlton. They will still he here waiting for you beside this telephone. Up to six o'clock, which is our closing time.'

Feeling slightly better, I ran back to the lounge, forcing my brain towards the next high hurdle.

'You are going to get there by what means?'

'There's one chance, Romesh. Just remembered what I spotted the other day. Up the hill. By the Lodge.' I stopped for breath.

'Tell.' His face told me he didn't want to know about hills. Or White Lodges. Just about transport.

'One set of wheels. They've left it lying idle, under a tarpaulin.'

I saw his lips start to suggest Hagemann, and began to walk. 'I'll get the heap going. You'll have those cassettes by three.'

He looked out and upwards, towards the suddenly pewter sky, measuring the light. I now had less than three hours.

There must have been something in my voice. He listened, and without a word, left me standing by the desk. Galore was back with the heavy can and the ring of keys inside a minute.

'It will save you breaking Mr St James's off-side window,' he told me, straight-faced, holding open his back door.

'And if you're lucky, he won't be back with us for a day or more.' It didn't make me feel any better.

The overgrown path from the back of the hotel wound through the sparse trees and damp grass at an angle which soon had me gasping. The only noises were the slopping of the petrol in the can and, further away and still higher, that sharp clack from the loose shutter. The path led steeply up to the unmade road which brought me to the white wooden gate in the white wooden fence. It was locked. The padlock and chain were new, but already reddish with rust stains.

The largest key fitted. I propped one of the many stones against the gate to hold it open for my fast departure for Stornoway.

It was a station-wagon. And also beginning to show rust, sea-salt rust, in spite of the taut tarpaulin. But, freed from its bonds, it guzzled the petrol I poured in. The sliding door responded to the second of the smaller keys and its engine talked back to me after three turns of the ignition.

It was that shutter which made me swing round and grope backwards to cannibalize string from the tarpaulin.

I had thrown it into the back of the station-wagon. My hand touched something soft but brittle in the shadows just behind the seat. Then something more solid, splintery and sharp. Cursing, I got out and unlocked the rear doors.

It was straw my fingers had first touched. And some scrunched-up newspaper. I noticed it was cheap tabloid. Then a piece of picture-frame. With flecks of gold leaf still sticking to the wood. I held it up and looked more closely, trying to reach back into my memory. To something half-recalled from a few days ago.

It came to me. The glossy auction-room catalogue in the hotel lounge. With the scrawled bid prices on each page. For the White Lodge, the cover had said. These scrambled facts added together in my mind to a sudden fear that we might not be the only people on the Isle of Lewis with an interest in the international art market.

There was also something about the locked-up house itself I didn't like. As if jeering at my fear, the shutter kept banging. I decided it was a feeling I would not yet share with Romesh.

I stopped staring at the padlocked front door. Its keys were, in any case, not on the ring in my hands. Now there wasn't even time to tie down a flapping shutter. I had to get to Stornoway. I shut the back doors, shivering in the sharper hillside wind, and jumped back inside the wagon I was about to steal. It had all lopped another ten minutes off a tight time-schedule. I hit the foot-pedals hard.

CHAPTER 15

The steering was the sort I like, stiff but accurate. But speed was what I really needed. I heaved the station-wagon round the first of the hundred bends. The tyres scarred the loose gravel of the unmade stretch of track but held the sharp curve down past the back of the hotel. Suddenly I was on the better, still narrow, road which curled up and out of Valtos. The steep, bare hills grabbed and twisted at the bitumen strip I was driving along. It gave split-seconds to react to anything coming the other way.

As the first car reared up at me, I remembered just in time that the tiny bulges on the single track were passing places.

Again and again I hit the pedal, making the vehicle roar forward off the top of every rise in the road. The villages, made up of houses scattered like thrown dice, sped past the side window. In between lay the wild scenery of west Lewis —a crazy-quilt of rock, boulders, and scree thrown by some giant hand trying to copy the landscape of the moon. It was half past twelve.

The road signs flashing by me were mostly in Gaelic. My brain was still struggling to translate into English by the time they vanished behind me. It didn't much matter; there was only the single road.

I roared on, cutting every corner, surging up every sharp incline, down every dip in the road.

I finally traced the scraping, metallic noise. With my free hand, I unclipped the glove compartment and rummaged inside. The sound stopped as soon as my hand touched the revolver. It was neat and nasty. And it was loaded. I tossed the weapon back. This time it fell silently. I reached inside and pulled out the papers which had muffled the fall. I stuffed the sheets into a pocket of my jacket and shut the compartment flap.

All at once the inside of the station-wagon exploded in a hellish death rattle. It had come from under me. Sweating, I looked in the rear-view mirror. I had just rocketed over a cattle-grid. I swallowed and drove on, pretending that I hadn't felt the sudden jolt of raw fear.

Sweeping round the next tight curve, I had to spin the steering-wheel sharply to avoid a side-swipe. The giant contractor's lorry lurched the other way, the driver cursing me silently from his high cab. Suddenly, to my right, were the neat lines of surveyors' posts—stuck in an elevated ramp of a road like so many burial crosses. It was a new road, not yet tarred; high and straight, above the narrow strip I was on. A huge earth-moving machine lay off to one side, pleased with the work it had done. I glimpsed the red sign whose twin I hadn't seen seconds earlier. It read BLASTING IN PROGRESS. No Gaelic. Behind me, through the back windows, I saw the cloud of dust my wheels had kicked up.

I was more than half way there. My watch digits said 12.55. The sprawl of rocks was gradually being broken by green daggers of boggy ground, barren, but holding out some hope to a hardy crofter. The red telephone-box by the roadside stuck out like a painted fingernail on a nun's hand.

The black road wove and buckled ahead. There were now no villages. I had left the edges of the sea lochs, speeding towards the tree-less, empty heart of the island. The odd pebble-dashed house lay in its own hollow, away from the winds of the approaching Hebridean winter.

Round the worst bend, the sun disappeared at a single blow from the speeding cloud-bank. Swearing, I flipped on side lights. Within a minute the first spatters of rain hit the windscreen and forced me to switch to headlights.

A sudden car—the first for miles—flashed its lights in my face, the steep road turning its dipped headlights into blinding beacons. I jerked the wheel sideways, feeling the judder as the nearside tyres sank into the peaty road-side.

I accelerated through the low-lying oasis called Gisla. Then along the hairpin which squeezed the road like black toothpaste round the last of the sea lochs, forcing it up and over the wet, slanting rock-faces.

There was no real chance to look into the rushing salmon streams of Grimersta. Or worry about the straying grouse as I swept past the new tree plantations of Garynahine. There the road doubled its width. I forced the engine above seventy, aiming all the while east, towards Stornoway.

It was now 1.40. I was whole minutes ahead of my urgent schedule. The rain stopped as I sped past the clumps of bright plastic bags full of freshly-cut peat, awaiting collection at the roadside. The sun came out. It was another typical Lewis day.

The trees told me I had reached the outskirts of the one town on the large island. The road skirted the edge of the Castle Grounds with the squat granite gatehouse and curved below the War Memorial, high on a hill overlooking the golf course, shielded by a scattering of wind-bent trees.

Almost too quickly, I was driving along the main street, passing the start of the sheltered harbour, towards the principal shopping area. The traffic going against me seemed wayward, determined to block my path. I braked sharply at the only parking sign I had seen that afternoon.

Finding the shop which stocked the videos took me longest. Out of breath, I ran back across the road to the car park with the tapes in one hand and the psychedelic Scottish pound notes which were my change in the other. I had been bloody rude to the owner, leaving him open-mouthed. His Stornoway accent, higher and faster than the voices I was getting used to on the Atlantic side of the island, still rang in my ears.

As I dodged between the shoppers, a gap in the angry, fast clouds threw sunlight on to the rigging of the trawlers nudging the sheltered inner harbour quay. I had a sudden thought of a bigger boat arriving that evening. But there was no time to wait for Sharmila and the divers. Besides, I had to be back in Valtos and filming that first slice of video action with Romesh and the appalling Hagemann.

The sun had gone again by the time I jumped back into my station-wagon. The way back was going to be easier, I told myself. I was now familiar with the route. I knew all the twists and turns. My nervous system could now even cope with the fright of the cattle grids. I could shave fifteen minutes from the first lap and still be back at the Loch Roag Arms by three o'clock.

But as the wagon swayed round the last bend and dropped into that giant hairpin at Gisla, I saw the other vehicle ahead of me. The fresh rainstorm battering at my windscreen was sending diagonal streaks across the side window. But I still saw enough to start sweating again. An identical station-wagon, long and low.

It was half a mile away—racing along the other arm of the hairpin. It couldn't be, I told myself. But what was it Galore had said in the hotel? I tried desperately to decide whether it was better to speed up or slow down, and suddenly remembered something else about the road ahead.

I tramped down again on the accelerator. I had my action plan.

Within a mile, I was tightly behind the other station-wagon, the one with the owner of my own transport inside. I prayed that he was a poor user of his rear-view mirror, then realized the layout of the island roads didn't encourage that sort of road-craft. And the rain was obscuring his view of me. There seemed to be more than one shadowy figure inside the dark interior, but it was impossible to be sure.

I cut my speed without falling too far behind. My plan depended on a sudden surge of power.

The roadworks sign I was looking out for came at me through the rain-furrowed windscreen like a red traffic-light. But my reactions now had to be positive. I rammed my right foot down to the floor and sent my wagon careering forward. I wrenched the steering-wheel hard left, slewing the vehicle upwards and sideways. Up and on to the new, unfinished surface which cut across the loop in the existing road. Up and forward, scattering the surveyors' posts to both sides or under my tyres. Startled workmen tumbled out of their roadside hut, tea spilling from their mugs.

This time, because of the rain, there were no clouds of dust to give me away. It prevented the people in the other van from seeing that they had been overtaken. The new, high-level track forced me into a wild skid on the downward slope back to the original roadway, ahead of my rivals. I didn't care. I was now well ahead, foot still flat on the van floor.

Twenty minutes later, now squinting into the western sun, I swung round the last, arm-aching bend, snatching a glimpse of the boats at the Valtos quayside below. There was no time for sight-seeing. With my free hand I reached behind me and grabbed an edge of tarpaulin. I lugged it on to the seat beside me, ready for my last fast action.

Swerving sharply left, my tyres hit the gravel of the Lodge's unmade road and hissed through the open gateway. I came to an abrupt stop outside the locked house. It now looked even more sinister, after what I had seen in the glove compartment.

I threw the tarpaulin over the body of my station-wagon and prayed the driver coming up behind me wouldn't think of feeling the engine-housing. I stopped tugging cord after I had lashed down three hurried corners. One loose tie wouldn't be noticed. Picking up the video cassettes, I just remembered to kick away the boulder holding open the gate.

I was half way down the slippery path to the back door of the Loch Roag when I heard the other engine, whining as it took the last, roughest, incline up to its home outside the White Lodge. In the same second, I remembered the petrol can I had thrown away. I ducked low and prayed. I kicked it into the ditch by the low wall and started to run.

My Monday had not been a complete write-off. It was five minutes past three and the sun had hit our small harbour yet again. There was light and time for a fast hour's film-making.

CHAPTER 16

Gulping in air, I stumbled and slithered down the path and through the door into the back of the Loch Roag. Taking the back stairs two at a time, I was clawing at the plastic wrapper on the first of the video tapes. I managed to pull it off at last, banged my bedroom door open with my shoulder, and started to pick up the video equipment and wetsuit. There was no time for a modest changing of gear.

Slowing down just long enough to dump the key-ring he had given me on Galore's desk, I was half way out of the empty office when I remembered my bright idea to make up for the missing oxygen cylinder for Hagemann's photogenic back. I reached up and pulled the fire-extinguisher off the wall.

I heard the engine of our boat in mid stride, racing down the path to the quay and pushing the video tape into its housing. I snapped shut the watertight casing around the camera as I ran up the gangplank. To be greeted by a Hagemann already rubber-suited and looking pointedly at his watch. Fortunately for him, I had neither fist free.

Romesh didn't smile in my direction either. He told me as the boat started off, 'We shall discuss first video shootings while travelling to diving location.'

Catching my breath, I stepped over some survey equipment they had laid out ready on the pitching deck. Doing that also stopped me from throwing a punch in a second direction. 'Right!' It wasn't worth saying anything more.

'I shall take up position in wheelhouse.' As Romesh said that, I saw for the first time that he had borrowed Hagemann's unwanted cap. It annoyed me even more than what he had just said.

'Right,' I said again. He blinked back at me, probably disappointed I hadn't said he looked terrific. Above us, a sea-gull cried out.

I talked rapidly to them both then, putting the camera to one side and struggling to get into my wetsuit. 'Look, you two, you both know what we need to do to make this bloody photo-opportunity work!' I jabbed a finger towards Hagemann. 'We need *you* to get down to that sea-bed bloody sharpish and look as if you were seeing these china chamber-pots for the very first time.'

Then I turned the same finger on Romesh. 'And we need to do that before we run out of light and before *your* daughter arrives with her gang to move the whole cargo sharpish back up to the surface!'

They took my outburst very well. Neither of them gave me an argument. Hagemann even let me strap the fire-extinguisher to his back without moaning, once I had per-suaded them that it would photograph just like the oxygen cylinder Gallacher had made off with.

Within two minutes we were at anchor above the diving site, hidden as usual from the shore by our little island. Both Hagemann and I were now masked and flippered. I was snorkeled, Hagemann having the harder job of holding his breath and pretending to get oxygen from a bright red fire-extinguisher. He had dropped the sarcastic half-sneer and was now intent on business; video business. I passed him the metal framework which held the lights.

Romesh went to pick up the 'stinger', the thin metal probe

which divers use to force silt and debris to one side. I grabbed his arm.

'Too bloody small to show up on a TV screen! We'll use the fat one, the airlift!'

My dander was still up. 'Start up the motor. Give him the nozzle end. We need something that'll come over really big, not a frigging electric tooth-pick!'

It didn't matter to me that one tool blew and the other sucked. It was the image I was shouting about.

The sudden shock that I was about to do it all the wrong way round hit me in my rubberized chest.

'The daylight!' I was shouting at Romesh again. He looked blank.

'Think about it! Another half-hour and it'll be as black up here as it is down on the sea-bed! We've got to fit in your gallant-captain bit before the light goes!'

I could feel my chest heaving inside the tight wetsuit.

Romesh blinked and spoke just one crisp sentence. 'I am now ready,' he told me. He stepped back into the wheel-house, his chin held at what he must have thought was the same heroic angle as Peter O'Toole's jawline in *Lord Jim*.

From then on I just pointed and shot, very fast, remembering to pan across from the wheelhouse towards the airlift's rattling machinery without getting any of the nearby island shoreline in the picture. Finally, I zoomed down to capture some foaming wave-crests. 'Part One in the can!' I told them and lowered the heavy camera.

My arms ached. And my nerves were still ragged. I tugged on the mask again, now really clammy inside my wetsuit, and turned towards the watching Hagemann. He saw my face and said nothing. Waddling like two ducks we made for the small ladder hanging over the side of the boat.

With the throb of suction from the airlift's elephant trunk ringing in our ears, Hagemann and I sat on our bottoms on the diving platform for one deep-breathing second, wiggled our flippered toes in the sea-water, then dropped down, down into the twelve-foot depth where all the porcelain lay begging to be re-discovered.

We jumped into the water together.

With a slow-motion struggle, Hagemann forced the framework holding the lights into the sandy bottom and began to position himself for the great 'find'. I crouched, eye on the eyepiece of the viewfinder, and raised my hand, ready to give a silent signal that I was ready to start shooting. We were straddling the longest row of half-buried porcelain.

A sign from Hagemann told me he had to go up for air. I followed, my snorkel tube making my return to the sea-bed faster than his.

As I turned the focusing ring for the first time I saw that he suddenly had a large white plastic bag tied to his weighted belt. It looked ridiculous—as if a huge blow-fish had taken him for a long-lost friend. He was now making more frantic, slow signs to me with the hand which wasn't on the nozzle of the airlift. I stopped, finger poised to shoot. Kicking out with his webbed feet to keep upright, Hagemann was struggling, nozzle now between his thighs, to undo the plastic bag. At last he unknotted it. Then he grabbed the tube of the airlift again, his other hand holding shut the plastic bag and waved at me to re-start. With a bad grace, and short of air, I gave my signal for him to start up the airlift.

At once the nozzle kicked into action and began to suck greedily at the sand around the rows of porcelain. Exactly at the time I started to shoot, Hagemann released the plastic bag. And immediately engulfed us both in a huge swirling cloud of tea leaves.

I cursed uselessly into my mouthpiece and switched off. Kicking out in fury, I shot to the surface, out of breath and angry. I pulled myself on to the diving grid platform and clambered up the steps of the short ladder to the deck, tearing the business-end of my breathing tube from my mouth.

'Romesh! Did you give him that sack of black crap to play with?' I could hear myself shout. 'Jesus Christ! That's all I need, short of shooting time and the man throws a bag of sheep-shit straight at my lens!' By that time, a red-gilled Hagemann had come up the ladder too and stood, shivering and dripping beside me. 'You've only buggered up our best set-piece, you two!' Gulping air, he stared at a shell-shocked Romesh.

Seconds passed. 'Nigel, show calmness, kindly.' He was not going to raise his voice to match mine. 'Tea-leaves are necessary prop. What do you imagine ancient Dutch seamen used as other valuable cargo in voyage from China? What material do you think kept porcelain safe from ravages of deep-sea currents?'

'Tea-leaves,' I said lamely and put down the heavy video camera.

'Exactly so. It is necessary backdrop to shooting. Will add realism. You will both recover collective breaths and submerge once more.'

I looked at Hagemann and he looked at me. I shouldered the camera a second time and let him slide into the sea ahead of me.

As I balanced on the edge of the grid, ready to jump, I felt an arm on the rubber shoulder of my suit. Romesh, without a word, pushed an ice-cold salmon under my elbow. He didn't need to explain. I was now into props. It was the fish Ginger had promised us from the hotel deep-freeze.

The filming went smoothly after that. Moving as fast as was possible in the water and coming up for air less and less often, Hagemann and I set ourselves up for all the vital shots. Hagemann manhandling the airlift to suck up the first debris from the long row of porcelain, ribs of worm-eaten hull in the background; a close-up of Hagemann holding up a tiny blue porcelain cup in triumph—eyes shining through the glass of his face-mask. Then two close-ups of a very dead salmon, pushed by our heroic diver and seeming to swim past an underglaze-blue saucer through a swirl of tea-leaves.

Altogether, we came to the surface five times, always giving Romesh the thumbs-up signal of progress. The last time, he didn't wave. Instead he threw towards us a bright-red plastic laundry-basket. Grabbing hold of the attached cord, Hagemann dived down again and, waiting for me to re-focus, began to pile plates, cups and saucers inside. Two tugs on the line attached and the filled basket floated weightily upwards towards the shadow of our boat.

I gave one last signal to Hagemann and we both kicked, following our treasure up to the surface. By that time, I was almost fond of him.

The light was now really dim. We packed the surveying gear and video equipment in the wheelhouse, ready for the next day. As I put the camera into its case, I noticed Romesh's bag. It was still locked. I had lost a bet with myself about when the mystery would unfold.

I left Hagemann and Romesh on board, still stacking and storing. I wanted to check—before they did—the results of my rushed shooting. In the colour monitor in my bedroom.

As I struggled on one leg to get out of my wetsuit, one foot on cold linoleum, for some reason I remembered what I had rescued from the glove compartment of the station-wagon.

Hopping over to where I'd thrown my jacket on to the coverlet, I pulled out the sheet of paper. I sat down damply on the edge of my bed.

It looked harmless enough. A leaflet on the historical churches of East Anglia. Only the notes in the margins of each page made me wonder. The writing was crabbed and nervy; difficult to read; bad-tempered. But it seemed clear enough—whoever was up at the Lodge was showing a great interest in religious art. But it wasn't adding up. A *Sun* and *Star* reader, fond of winkles and whelks, with an overweening interest in church art? And living in the White Lodge surrounded by Calvinists? I would have to go back up the hill. And the return of the man Grass and his customers had nicknamed 'St James' meant that I had a far more difficult task ahead of me if I wanted to see the inside of that locked-up house.

'Nigel! Dormobile. It has arrived!' I shoved aside thoughts of dinner.

Anyway, I had been concentrating on the screen of my TV monitor. It was all coming together. Apart from the need to re-sequence the shots of Romesh, nothing else called for an edit. Even the jerkiness of my camerawork made for an authentic, hand-held look to the pictures. Deep-sea treasure-hunting at its most photogenic. Hangemann, I had to admit, looked good—properly excited by his sudden lucky find. The logistics showed up well; and good grainy background images of the ribs of a Dutch East Indiaman. I had even worked in a close-up of the Gopal-drilled worm-holes in the hull. And our lights gave the illusion of working underwater at a far greater depth. There had been no boo-boo's of accidental snatches of nearby dry land, or of a survey boat a mere twelve feet above the sea-bed. Even Captain Romesh looked properly nautical at his wheel. Everything I had shot that late afternoon had worked. All it needed, to make it snappy for the media, was a quick edit.

'Nigel! Dormobile! It is now with us!' I moved that second time and switched off the set.

From my high window, I looked down as two of the Gopal team of divers jumped down from their vehicle and began to pull gear out through the back doors. A radiant girl was leaning out, waving to her father.

I stepped outside just in time to hear Sharmila try to console him. 'Really sorry, Dad,' she was saying as she tried to wrap her arms round his wide waist. 'Poor old Dad! All his first bit of video finished hours ago. Then he has to twiddle his thumbs while his beautiful daughter boogies towards him across that bog, late as hell. We just couldn't make it on to that first ferry-boat, Dad! Chock-a-bloody-block.'

'Exactly so,' he told her, smoothing his thick hair as if we hadn't finished one late, gut-busting shooting schedule ten minutes before she'd turned up.

The air he sucked in this time was self-righteous.

'Nevertheless, young lady, we can forgive both lateness and language. That is so, is it not, Mr Carlton?'

As he turned towards me, she stepped across and planted a smacking kiss on my cheek. Romesh frowned.

Any ensuing embarrassment was cut short.

'Mr Gopal!' It was Galore, shouting from the hotel doorway, telephone receiver in his outsized hand. 'You should know that they have heard of your find. The Lord knows how.'

Romesh's brow creased.

'The journalists, Mr Gopal! They have somehow found you out, I am sorry to say. There is a newspaper man setting out first thing tomorrow morning from Stornoway. They are on to you.'

CHAPTER 17

Up in my room with the door locked, I was editing video tape. Fast. The next day all hell would break loose. There would be a second bout of filming at an even greater pace than today—this time starring Sharmila and her team. Romesh had just told us all that we would have to move at speed, great speed, from 8.0 a.m., to finish off the underwater video sequences and pull up all the goodies—without breakages—from the sea-bed. By moving so quickly, a certain unwanted, ahead-of-Gopal-schedule reporter would see only what he was supposed to see. That is, porcelain being washed lovingly and carefully, having been ferried back from the depths of the far Atlantic, twelve and one-half miles out from the coast of Lewis. In other words, no newspaper snooper was to see that our underglaze-blue had only moments before rested in just two fathoms of sea-water, five minutes' sailing from the Valtos quay.

So, on that next morning, I would barely have time to let my flippers touch water before surging back up to the surface and drying off both myself and the porcelain.

Hence the need for a speed-up that evening. I knew too that the next evening would almost certainly be taken up in regaling the pressman with stories of a surprising, non-oilbearing find. And the whole of the day after that would be devoted to the Great Treasure Exposition in the hotel.

With all that hyper-activity coming up, the only time-slot I had to break into a certain puzzling White Lodge was that night. Immediately after I had performed my video chores.

There was one other item of news driving me on. Passing the open doorway of the bar, I had overheard Galore tell his barman to be sure to check his supply of London gin. They were expecting the people from the Lodge. Grass had made a sarcastic joke to his boss on the chance of being bought a round by St James.

Galore had then ordered his chief glass-polisher to be civil the next day to a visiting pressman. Again it sounded as if our normally-placid host had little respect for the man from the *Stornoway Free Press*. I felt I still didn't know the full reason for that.

After half an hour's concentration, I snapped the cover back on to my video-edit machine and stored away the master tape. I changed into my darkest sweater and trousers. My once-white joggers would not be reflecting much light either. I put the rubberized torch in my hip pocket and checked that I had my broad-bladed knife with me.

Moving down the back stairs, feet on the outer sides of every creaky step, I next edged past the bar doorway. No one inside was worrying about my after-dinner absence. All eyes were on Sharmila's sparkly top. I could hear Romesh begin to josh Grass on his latest choice of trendy green clothing. Even Hagemann's shoulders heaved with pretended good humour.

Nearer the door was what I really hoped to see. Two new silhouettes against the lights behind the drink bottles. The two men were talking to each other in low voices, one half-turned towards the Gopal drinking party. I thought I recognized the shape of a back from the station-wagon I had overtaken that afternoon. The Lodge would now, I was gambling, be empty for at least an hour.

The sharp Hebridean moonlight wasn't helping me. I could already see it, bouncing off the painted boards of the Lodge far above me, like a disco spotlight. My shadow, tiptoeing across the gravel to attack the lock on the front door, would be trapped in the white light and pinned like a butterfly. Stepping up the slanting path from the hotel, I decided instead to go for the window with the lame shutter. At least then, if there was someone else inside, any noise I would make might be put down to the banging wood. There were no lights anywhere on the long, low side of the house. And no sound, except for the nerve-jangling clack.

The window-catch slipped sideways on my first hack at

it with my knife-blade. In seconds I was standing on the bare floorboards of the unused bedroom. Stock still. There were no sounds from inside the Lodge, no light under the door. In the dark, wide corridor, I flicked on my torch. I could smell the sea-damp in the wooden walls. And still only one noise.

Creeping to the end of the passage, I opened one side of the double doors. It took me into the biggest room in the house. My torch-beam lit up an amazing, multi-coloured scene. On all sides of the room, paintings of every size stared back at me. Every one in heavy oils. Of dark and gloomy religious subjects.

The gold on the broad gilded frames shone dully in my torchlight. Frame after frame. I swept the beam around the wide room. I was surrounded by church art. I stepped nearer. Behind every oil painting stood another—they had all been stacked on edge on the carpeted floor. To my left lay carved altarpieces. Over the back of a low sofa to the right were various wall-hangings, piled on top of each other. I pulled a wooden slab forward to see what was behind, and felt the sharp stab of a nail. And another. I ran my hand across the back of the next wood-carving. More rusty nails. Pieces of loose plaster fell on the floor at my feet. The wooden sculptures had been wrenched from church mountings.

In the middle of the room, on a Persian carpet, lay a pile of crate panels. And hammers and nails and a pair of heavy-duty pincers. And more crunched-up tabloids, ready for packing. The work was in full swing. I had stumbled into a Hebridean Aladdin's Cave.

One of the crates was nearly made up. I dropped on one knee and read the name and London address of what could have been an art-dealer. It was not a firm I knew. I shut the twin door quietly, listening for the click of the catch.

The kitchen told me more. It was used exclusively by males, to judge by the upheaval and the unwashed, scattered dishes. The new smell was of stale cooking fat. The next room was the main bedroom. And more facts I could do without.

Even in the waning beam from my torch, the all-black décor was strong. It matched the black curtains and bed-covers. There was also something weird about the way the twin beds had had their stubby legs lashed together with heavy cord.

Hanging from a framework above the beds was a thrown-back mosquito net. I was baffled—then remembered the curse of the Hebridean summer: the midges. They were taking good care of themselves.

I opened up the tall wardrobe. The first heavy wood door swung aside slowly. To show me a full-length photographic blow-up of two men embracing. A brutal, explicit, naked grabbing. And to the inside of the other door someone had taped a poster of a stripped and bound boy. On his bare left buttock was a small symbol. I craned forward. It was a swastika. I had stumbled on something more than a treasure cave.

The sudden noise from outside was not of shutter hitting frame.

I snapped off the torch, opened up my knife-blade, and stepped quickly back into the central corridor.

The sounds got nearer; they were human noises. Plus one other. It started as a whine; then a lower-pitched noise, just audible. The strained growl of a big dog. As if the beast was pulling against a strong, short lead. I should have looked down at the floor as I passed the door to the bar in the Loch Roag.

Then came the worst sound. Of claws against the wood of the front door. I flattened my spine against the wall, moved rapidly away from that end of the corridor, and backed into the main room. I shut the twin doors as sound-lessly and securely as I could. There was no key.

Like most satisfied drinkers, they made straight for the kitchen. I heard tins being overturned, then opened. And crude talk, somehow gloating. Then came the animal's claws again, first on the floorboards along the side of the corridor, then scratching at the double doors.

I dropped down on to the grass outside the long front of the house, and pulled shut the main window which had been my exit route. The moon was now working even more strongly against me, but it did show up something I had missed on my way in—the kennel with the chain hanging from the iron ring.

Chest heaving, I crept carefully down the four steps leading to the steep path down to the hotel. Behind me, all that I could hear was that shutter flapping again in a sudden gust of cold wind. It seemed to be laughing at me.

'So where have you been, Wallflower?'

She was posed prettily against the upright of my bedroom door, a glass in each hand, the flat of one raised shoe against the wood. Someone had told Sharmila I now drank whisky.

'Out on the tiles. And chasin' Mary Flora across the moor, I suppose. Obviously likes her men long and thin and sexy.'

I looked up from my edit machine. I had just had time to open it up before I had heard her heels on the stairs.

'Had to press on. Doing the boring bit,' I lied. 'Sorry about missing out. Put it down to your Old Man and his tight work schedule.' I managed to say it all without sounding out of breath.

'Came up half an hour ago, but you weren't in, Nige.'

I couldn't quite tell from her face. The gaze was level, her expression dead-pan.

'Out huntin', weren't you?'

She put my glass down on the bedside table and sat on the edge of my bed.

'Tried to get you as soon as these two creeps in black leather down in the bar started the verbal abuse bit on poor old Dad and the boys.'

She looked up at me.

'What?'

'These two from the house up the hill. Once they'd got tanked up, they started edging down the bar, didn't they? Upset Rajat's drink, very accidentally—only their ugly Cockney mugs didn't look like they were sorry.'

She took a shaky sip at whatever clear stuff she had in her glass.

'You mean these villains from the White Lodge were trying to mix it with our lot? Racially?'

'Not just racially, Nige. They were also after the reason for us bein' up here. Seemed to know quite a lot as it was, the bastards. White Lodge! What a name! Why weren't you here, Nige?'

'Sharmila, I wasn't—'

'OK. You haven't made the maid. So you said. But you weren't around when I really needed you, Nige. I'm not pullin' your leg this time, you know.'

Suddenly I wasn't proud of lying to her about my absence. 'Let's go down now,' I told her.

'You're too late. They went off when that man-sized landlord showed up. Sneerin' and laughin' up the sleeves of their bomber jackets, they were. God! I'd just like to have kneed the old one in his scrawny leather crutch!'

'They didn't . . .? You're . . .?'

'Ignored me completely. Looked straight through as if I didn't exist. Really creepy, that was. Worse than what they were doin' to the boys. And Dad.'

'Romesh's all right?'

'As usual. You know him. Bounced back exactly one

minute after the sods left us in peace. He doesn't know I'm up here, mind you. Thinks I'm already tucked up in my little bedroom.'

I decided not even to hint about my own fears brought down from the hill. 'What does he think these two will be up to tomorrow?'

'Not the aggro bit. You can see what's really worryin' him is whether they aim to screw up his scam. What if they suss us out, Nige?'

I didn't know the answer to that. Instead, another thought came to me. 'Where was Hero Hagemann when all this was going on?'

She snorted. 'He'd gone off just after you, Nige. With an even wetter excuse. Needed his sleep, he said.' She snorted again. 'Two hunky Brits on the team and neither of them anywhere around when the nasties turn up! One good thing though, accordin' to Dad.'

'Tell me.'

'Well, he was really glad that reporter hadn't arrived to drop his eaves when these Fascist bastards started quizzin' us. Anyway, he's back to his old form, orderin' me up the stairs to get my head on the pillow, ready for the early-off tomorrow. You're in charge, incidentally. So he says.'

I straightened my shoulders. 'You'd better clutter off then, young lady.'

'What?' she asked, looking upwards at my mouth. 'With me in my best ball-gown?'

'Cut that out,' I told her. 'You're supposed to be in bed. Your bed.'

She lay back on both elbows, her bust surging forward and sparkling in the light from my bedside lamp.

'*Your* bed,' I said it again, not quite so masterfully.

But some of the conviction must still have been there. She straightened her half-naked back, drained her glass and wiped the lipstick from the edge, then put it back next to mine. She stretched sleepily.

'So what are you goin' to do to kill the rest of the night off, Nige—flatten the heather one more time with Mary Flo'?'

'I'll be downstairs calling London,' I told her almost truthfully. 'Checking out a name with a friend of mine in the art business.'

'Give her my love, or whatever.' She got up, blew me a silent kiss and walked out. The door closed softly behind her.

CHAPTER 18

'Up, up, up! Everybody up!'

I shouted it out at exactly 7.30 a.m. as I marched through the bedroom door and stumbled against the end of her bed.

But she was already up. And washed and dressing-gowned. Her naked face was about to receive the full treatment. She put down the hand-mirror and the blusher and waited for me to become vertical.

'Somebody eaten your porridge, Nige?'

The tiny room was the last in the place, Galore had told her father. I looked around and goggled.

Romesh's locked bag sat, squat and heavy, by the window.

She saw my face. 'You'll have to leave the two of us now, Nige.' She paused for effect. 'Me and the bag, I mean. Got to unleash the family jewels.'

There was a faint metallic clunk as she lifted the bag on to the bed. I left the room a lot less confident than when I'd gone in.

*

'Down, down, down! Everybody down!'

Half an hour later I was trying to force enthusiasm and speed into the rest of the Gopal diving team. And being a lot more successful. One after the other the skinny brown men shivered, then flipped off the diving platform into the water and down to the sea-bed a dozen feet below. I followed after a last sight of Hagemann's bare chest.

The creep was not due to be filmed that morning; his turn was over. And it was not exactly sub-tropical in the wheelhouse on board the *Girl Mairi*. To add to my annoyance, he had put on his best, pressed trousers and the peaked cap. It was all aimed at having an effect on Sharmila. And it had worked.

'Wow! Look at that man, Nige!' she had breathed out of the corner of her mouth.

'How many "s"s are there in narcissistic?' I asked her.

She too had spent some extra time in front of her wardrobe that early morning. She wore a fluffy angora top which picked up every colour in the Hebridean seascape. And there were no spare inches to leave anyone in doubt about the structure beneath the wool. Her tight black leotard bottoms set off the riot of subdued blues, purples, and greens on her upper half. Only irritation at her interest in our part-time pilot stopped me from really enjoying it.

I dropped over the side, camera balanced on my left shoulder.

The divers performed quickly, perfectly. It was probably the water temperature rather than my shouting which got them to move. Whatever, they weaved and bobbed, swooped and twisted around the sea-bottom like a school of young porpoises. I captured every loading of porcelain into the plastic baskets. By the time I had taken enough shots of dinner plates and tea-bowls and saucers with the appropriate backdrops of floating tea-leaves, sunken hull, or half-thawed salmon, almost all of our brittle cargo had been hoisted on board the boat above our heads.

Back on deck, I wiped my camera casing dry and looked at my watch. 'Now they have to pull the rest out, double-quick,' I told Sharmila. 'Before the press-gang gets here from Stornoway.'

She shouted the two rapid orders over the rail in what must have been Bengali. Soon the water was boiling in a flurry of snorkel tubes, plastic buckets and dripping china. Within twenty minutes, all our great store of porcelain which had been sunk two whole days ago was up on that small, pitching deck.

Something made me look round at the deck. Among all the splashing, Sharmila had knelt down and was quietly unwrapping the folded headscarf she had brought on board. Inside, nestling between the silk folds, I saw the two neat blocks of solid gold.

It was what Romesh had been humping around the Hebrides all these days and not telling me about. She placed them next to the nearest row of glistening tea-bowls within her reach.

'For the Gents of the Press, Nige. You can look but not touch.' She raised a finger.

The blocks were an odd shape. I asked her why.

'Because Dad got Rajat to melt down his gold to look really old *and* Chinese. They get called "shoes", shaped like that, he says. Always have liked visitin' shoe shops, Nige—now I know why.'

She giggled, then threw me a mock-serious frown. 'Go on, point your lens at my best bits of footwear, then.' She was still enjoying herself.

I did what she said, then left her. I had to get on with something else vital—getting on to tape the washing-off operation by the team.

They were getting down to the task; bending over the

mass of buckets, basins, and mops we had rounded up from the giggling hotel maids the previous evening. My camera zoomed in on their bright rubber gloves as they scrubbed carefully away at each precious item. Finally happy that I had got enough treasure-retrieval on to video-tape, I headed up the hill and into the lobby of the Loch Roag. I had a London call to make.

She wasn't there. It was 9.15 a.m. Greenwich Mean Time and Caroline hadn't got to Carruthers & Co. yet. I told them no, I would ring her later, rather than the other way round.

As I jumped back on board, frustrated, the youngest diver shattered two cups against the side of the boat. I smiled at him. He was carrying out Romesh's earlier instruction. We needed something that was less than perfect from our dredging operation.

Carefully sprinkling the broken pieces among the rest of the porcelain, I had to step over the gold shoes. She was watching every move I made. And had an answer to my unasked question.

'Not until Rupert Murdoch's mate has seen them, Dad reckons. Just as soon as his eyes get back inside their sockets and he jots it down in his notebook, I plonk the shiny stuff back in Dad's bag and lock it.' I shrugged, still hurt that the Gopal family had cut me out.

'Aaahhh!' It was a colossal, wide-open yawn. 'Tell of progress, kindly,' he asked me.

I gave Romesh a rapid account of the morning.

'You are more concerned about something else, Nigel. I can see this in your face.' He was now fully awake.

He hadn't asked me about my previous day, let alone night. As he sat there, I told him all about the Stornoway run. He seemed more interested in the road and the road-

signs than my hectic race against the gang in the other
station-wagon. That annoyed me. He fell silent again, pulling thoughtful faces while I talked him through the layout
and creepy contents of the White Lodge. Then he spoiled it
all again by asking a footling question about where the
quarry was that I had gunned past.

He didn't seen to notice my abrupt reply.

'And Caroline was not there to answer query concerning
London art-dealing company?'

'They expect her to come in half way through the morning. Out on an evaluation, they said.'

He got up from the wooden edge of the boat. 'Then we
shall proceed as intended. It is more important that we pay
attention to fast-approaching media-man. We must not be
stampeded into rushed Gopal Treasure Exposition.' I had
wondered about the official title. I snorted.

He looked at his watch. 'We must have completed all
hoisting on to deck by time reporter appears. Has careful
washing-down of china commenced?' He asked it sharply.

I gave him an update. And just happened to mention
that I had seen some gold.

He hardly blinked. Instead, he said, 'And where is gold?'
More sharply.

'Dear Sharmila's got her left stiletto on it. Won't let
anyone else near it. Even me.' He ignored that too.

I scowled at him.

We marched off in our different directions, Romesh to see
beloved, trusted daughter; I to check that the diving team
didn't finish their crockery-cleaning operations before the
pressman arrived.

When I came back round the wheelhouse, Sharmila was
sitting on the edge of the hold armed with a tube of Super-
glue. Her long, thin fingers were moving at an amazing
speed. She was sticking shells decoratively on to one of the

half-dozen plates her father had grabbed from a diver.

'Nige, you're not busy. Be a love. Go for a paddle and bring me back some more of these thingies. The mankier the better.'

I realized then what she was up to—to look deep-sea genuine, some of our plates needed to have been taken over by creepie-crawlies in their two hundred years below the rollers of the North Atlantic. I clomped off, my wetsuit suddenly feeling like maximum overkill.

He turned up as the team started to toil up the path from the quay with the first of the rescued porcelain. They were about to go on full display.

For a reporter, he seemed too big. Over six foot two, my height, with hands and feet and hair to match his size. The tweedy hat was tilted at a Fleet Street angle on the back of his head, though, and his first question was properly ambiguous.

'Roddy Macleod. *Stornoway Free Press*. A good season for the poaching, wouldn't you say, Mr Carlton?'

He was already staring at the laid-out pieces still on the deck. And the gold shoes.

I grunted at him but stayed silent.

'I hear that I need not have rushed over.' I raised an eyebrow at him. 'There is to be a grand demonstration for the press, your landlord tells me. Reluctantly as ever. All tomorrow morning, he says. In his best reception room. In which case, I might as . . .'

His eyebrow went up too.

I was happy to help him.

'Grab yourself a malt and watch us from the picture window? It's warmer up there, actually.'

'That is exactly what I shall do, Mr Carlton!' The speed with which he accepted the suggestion and strode back up the hill was amazing. One minute later I saw him again, through the glass, bottom planted on the broad window-sill, a full glass raised in salute.

'Who told pressman to come from Stornoway?'

'If you ask me, it was either Galore or one of those old buffers chasing salmon every day.'

'Not Galore,' Romesh replied. 'He strongly dislikes.'

'Then it's either Fred or his dancing partner.'

'But little harm has been done, Nigel. He has seen porcelain wet from washing and coming up hill. And Chinese shoes of gold?'

I nodded. 'Not as impressed as all that. Decided it was warmer beside the peat fire.'

It was time someone supervised the laying of the porcelain on the shelving Romesh and Hagemann had set up in the hotel's biggest reception room. They had copied, on a smaller scale, the layout of the Christie's Amsterdam presentation they had seen in the Hatcher book. Romesh had torn out the page and taken it north.

By the time I came into the room, Sharmila was in complete control.

'Up there, between the two big plates, Rum-Jum!' she shouted at her fattest cousin. He was swaying on one short leg, half way up the ladder.

'Not there, Ashok! Looks terrible! Over that way. Against the bluey one, stupid! . . . Better! Definitely better.' She brushed dark hair out of one eye and turned round.

I had to tell her that her special display shelf was terrific. It showed off the most attractive dinner plates and our one soup tureen. She had filled three sides of the large room with china goodies, leaving the central area for her father to shine in the next day.

I watched the laying out on the plain, wooden shelves for a few more minutes, then looked at my watch. As I left the room, the big reporter passed me, going in. He had to sidestep, stomach sucked in to pass.

I waited for all the British Telecom clicking noises to die down.

'You're a fully paid-up Crumb-bum, Carlton. A louse.'

'There just aren't any postcards up here, Kay. End of the Western World.'

'So what have you been doing, Playboy? And who to?'

'I've been darned busy, if you must know. And Rubbish has more plans up his dhoti for—'

'So you won't be back for a while? Why didn't you ring me earlier? You've got no excuse, Carlton. The Scots invented the goddam telephone, after all. Alexander Graham Bell. In eighteen hundred and whatever.'

It was the second time I'd heard that.

'No. Sorry, Kay. Look, I'll be back by the end of the week. What I'd like you to do before that is—'

'Ah.' Without expression.

I spoke into the void. 'It's actually a very simple thing, Kay. It's . . . Kay, are you still there? . . . Kay?'

'I'm still here, Toad.'

'Anyway, Kay, it's just that I need someone who really knows the art—'

'Just get on with it, without the bullshit.'

'Allen, Farncombe & Freeson. Name mean anything to you?'

'Did. Rings a vague bell. Usually that means bad news. Anyway, I'm talking about yonks ago, Carlton. Could all be different now.'

'Right. Can you get me an update? Talk to your friend Julian, or whoever.'

'Maybe, Carlton. Why?'

'Please, Beautiful One.'

'OK. But you'll have to leave it with me. Not just at your beck and telephone call, you know.'

'I'll phone you again, Kay. Tonight.'

'Not going to give me the reason, then?'

'Tonight, depends on what you tell me.'

'Got to go. Work. Might have something for you by nightfall, if you're lucky. Just don't give me the Alexander Graham too early. Out to dinner. You're not the only man in my life, Carlton.' The way she said it told me differently. I rang off. Pleased but not pleased.

She was locking the door to the reception room. 'That newsman's quite a sweetie, really, Nige. Almost as terrif as Hagemann.' She giggled at my face. 'Your Ace Reporter knows just a bit about deep-sea divin' too. I'd be careful what I said. Off to warn Dad about that, matter of fact. Might have to change the spiel in his Media Show.'

Sharmila and I went together. Romesh was bending Galore's ear.

'. . . it was perhaps one of them who did so?'

'I would hazard such a guess, Mr Gopal. But it is no more than that.'

Galore started to leave. 'And I will check that the representatives of the English press will be on hand for you tomorrow morning.' He went off. I thought he was grinning to himself.

'Who did he reckon it was?'

'He wonders if source of information to newspaperman was one of old fishing men.'

'Well he would, wouldn't—' I didn't get time to finish.

'Dad! You've got to watch it, this press thing tomorrow. That newshound isn't as simple as he sounds. Not at all. Really clued-up about his sort of sea-water. Started askin' me all sorts of questions. Had to shut him up. With my eyelashes.'

Romesh blinked at her.

'That is other good reason why you must stay with us for some while longer, young lady.'

'Dad, I *promised* the boys we'd all be back . . .'

'You will suspend departure from island to coincide with that of Mr Carlton and me. You are needed for artistic skills as well as ability to charm pressmen.'

'But Dad, I *said* . . .!' Next week I go off to Portugal! I haven't bought one . . .!'

'Sharmila!'

She stabbed her toe into the floor a second time and tossed black hair at us.

But it didn't last.

'Oh, all right. But I'll have to take time off to see to the boys' packin' up. They're dead keen to get back to Eastern civilization—what with havin' to kip on the floor of the Dormobile and do without chicken biryani for the last four days. And when do I give my little lads their money?'

Romesh ignored the question about wages for his divers.

'You may tell them they can stay tonight in Stornoway. There they may obtain some Muslim cuisine.'

'They're going to love you for that.'

Romesh's neck bulged. 'It is better than roast beef!'

From then on, Sharmila didn't argue.

Suddenly she made for the door.

'Nige,' she wheedled, 'come out here with your still camera. Want you to take the team photo before the boys swan off. It'll be a souvenir for them from the Furthest North. I'll sit in the middle and hold somebody's ball.'

She started to push forked fingers through her hair, then smiled over-sweetly at us both.

CHAPTER 19

I was clambering over the power leads of the TV monitor and my playback machine when I heard the happy noises. Stepping round the longest rack of neatly-stacked porcelain, I looked out of the window of the hotel reception room and saw that Romesh and Sharmila were saying goodbye to the diving team. Sharmila had slung a wetsuit over one shoulder. As the Dormobile swung out of sight, she turned and winked at me. I went back to my electrical preparations for the great Gopal Treasure Exposition.

'Nice meal?'

'Not bad, McCarlton. Not bad at all. The company was good too.'

I let that pass. 'Kay, what did you find out?'

'Bad news. Or good, depending. You still haven't said why—'

'Just tell me.'

'Well, A.F. & F. deal on the fringe of the trade. The dodgy fringe. They specialize in religious. Nobody's been jailed yet, but they've been known to polish the odd provenance. So Jeremy tells me.'

'Polish? Provenance? Remind me.'

'Got a name for bending the facts on where they got their latest master-carving from—that's what he means. Just a bit. Here and there. Nobody really honest in the business buys their church stuff from them any more. They leave it for the punters to snap up.'

'Right.'

'Does that monosyllable mean you're not going to tell me why you wanted me to find out so rapidly, Carlton?'

'I'll pass the news on to Romesh. He was about to . . .'
I let it trail off.

'You mean all that was for your hare-brained boss? I
thought you two were too busy parting the Jocks from their
property at knock-down prices.'

I began to wonder whether I'd dug myself into a hole.
'You know he likes to think ahead, Kay. It was for when he
gets back. Wanting to expand into art. Wanted, rather. Past
tense.'

'You've got there at last, Carlton. Tell Sir to give A.F. &
F. a miss. They would take him to the cleaners. And I don't
mean picture restorers.' Silence fell. 'I've got to go. Feed
Rupert. You remember Rupert?'

'I remember Rupert.' My painful cat-food fracas came
back to me. 'Thought he'd just padded out with you for
that meal.'

'Wrong again. We're both due out on the tiles again later
tonight, matter of fact. Separately. *Ciao.*'

The rapid ending left me to wonder if my faked reason
for finding out about Allen, Farncombe & Freeson had
passed the Caroline litmus test.

As I walked back through the hall, my ribs were jabbed by
a black rubber arm.

'Like it, Nige? Good if you're into strict discipline.' She
looked amazingly sexy but I wasn't going to tell her that.
One thing spoilt it. The voice was suddenly very nasal.

'Say that again with the porthole open.'

She pulled the mask off.

'God! That's a relief! Wasn't meant to wear gas-masks!'
She tried to shake her hair, forgetting it was still inside the
rubber balaclava.

I looked her over and suddenly realized. 'Have you got
anything on under . . .?'

''Course not. Ashok's two inches smaller than me, isn't

he? All round.' She put a protective hand over the shiny outlines of her nipples.

'All round is right.'

'Shut up! Didn't tart myself up just to get ogled.'

But she wasn't too horrified.

'Will this do for Dad's Expo?' she asked. 'The idea is I stand up and wave at the pressmen when he snaps his fingers. Adds impact, he says. What do you think?' She dropped the hands, spread her arms straight out, and spun round on a black high-heel. She had left off the flippers.

I didn't get to answer the tricky question.

'Nigel, I have had additional concept.'

He had started talking almost before he came within range. 'We need not only TV video presentation to back up exposition. Blow-up photographs too are required. Blow-ups. You have been taking still pictures also, Sharmila tells.'

I glared at her in thanks, then turned back. 'They're private. For my album. Not for photo-montage.'

'Then we can use tomorrow. Blown up.' Romesh's face changed as he finished the sentence. He actually giggled as he said it. Then, just as quickly, he became serious again.

I didn't see the joke, if there was one. 'Haven't got the gear to—'

'You will kindly develop. Mr Galore has development facilities—to flatter fishermen with large catches. Kindly produce giant photographs this evening. I wish tomorrow to be blow-up day, Nigel.' He giggled again to himself.

I argued for two more minutes about technicalities, and lost. I had meant to bend his ear about the bad news from Caroline. But being forced into the hotel darkroom made me bloody-minded. I was damned if I was going to warn him about anything.

The room was too small; the shades to the lights too low for my head. But I had soon mastered the controls on the enlarger and run off the necessary photographs for him. It also gave me the chance to sharpen my fears about the people from up the hill.

The worst thought had hit me with full impact as I unlocked the darkroom. Caroline had said church art. That meant Catholic art. Certainly not Presbyterian Church art. It didn't exist. So why were they in the Outer Hebrides, North Chapter? If the stuff had been honestly got hold of on the Isle of Lewis—which was highly unlikely—it would have come from the Catholic churches of the southern half of the long chain of the islands—Benbecula, South Uist, or Barra. St James and his friend were up to something. Sending their stolen art back to London through Stornoway must mean they were covering their tracks. Probably A.F & F. would tell their buyers down south that Lewis was the local market centre.

Only there was no local art market. But nobody would be making the awkward journey from London to check it out. And, if their treasure trove was ever chanced upon, no Lewis Calvinist would realize the stuff was church art. Neat. And, for Romesh and me, dangerous. Too many crooks for the good of our own Scotch broth.

As I lifted the last dripping enlargement out of the developer, I heard the laughter from the bar. I speeded up, keen not to miss two drinking sessions in two days. I pinned the giant photographs to the back wall of the reception room, directly under Romesh's two baize-covered tables. We were set for tomorrow's grand exposition of the Gopal Treasure.

There were three groups under the low ceiling. At the back of the bar, Fred and Ginger sat at their usual table, deep in a discussion of the day's catch. At the far end, by the window, the reporter's bottom was overspilling his high stool. He was talking to the barman. Grass was laughing back at some low-volume Hebridean joke. He came down to my end of the bar, polishing the counter as he went. He was in green again.

'I'll have a Glen . . .'

'And I'll have another Clan Ding-dong at the same time, Nige. Just to keep you company!' She said it over Hagemann's navy tailored blazer shoulder. And then she giggled.

'Where's your father?'

'And Mr Hagemann—' her lovely brow creased—'is a rum, Nigel Carlton. Naval rum. Note the spelling, N-A-V-A-L.' She put her hand up to her mauve-shaded mouth again.

'And one Lamb's,' I told Grass. 'The young lady will not be having—'

'Kill-joy Carlton! Anybody ever call you that? Or is it a spot of rust in the old sporran?'

She made to jab a finger, low down. I stepped back. Into Romesh's stomach.

'You have had sufficient, Sharmila!' He said it sharply.

Holding high Hagemann's new drink, I smiled sweetly as I leaned across her. 'Blab!' she hissed in my ear.

'You have completed development, Nigel?'

I explained to him I had already pinned them up.

'And you locked door?'

'Of course.' I didn't remember for sure, but I wasn't about to tell him that.

We started to talk again of our lucky, end-of-season find; just loud enough to carry to the reporter's hair-filled ears. The idea was that he would walk over and join in our chat. Our good cheer was real. And Sharmila being there helped. That evening she was wearing a green, sequinned jacket. Below the padded shoulders, a deep V was outlined by more sequins in light blue. They sparked and danced each time she laughed.

Suddenly the sequins stopped moving. I looked into her

face. She was staring over my shoulder, towards the main door to the bar.

''Evenin', Grassie. How's tricks with you tonight?' I half-turned.

The wiry little man had come straight to the only gap behind me in the bar. He had already put his black leather elbow on the wet Formica. The height of the counter made the bottom of the tight blouson rise a couple of inches. I saw the key-ring dangling from his waist. The blond, short-cut head was turned away, towards his companion. The other man's moustache was also fine-clipped, but darker. He was taller. He was weighing up the people in the bar for his friend. I couldn't catch what he was whispering; the whines from the dog prevented that.

Sharmila had seen the animal too. She was straight-faced, all laughter gone. Hagemann continued to drink his rum, seemingly oblivious. I said something marginal, to fill in the silence, but no one was listening.

Instead, Grass hissed, 'St James,' at me, needlessly.

Romesh had put down his beer and squared his shoulders. The voice was designed to carry.

'You are wrong, Nigel. It is homosexual tendencies I abhor most strongly. They are true parasites of society. They make no family contribution.'

He picked up his straight-sided beer glass again. 'And it is easy to detect. There are special signs which they employ among themselves. You can tell at once.'

He was staring at the set of keys.

I had begun to edge round between Romesh and Sharmila to leave room for swinging my right arm, if needed. The men had stopped talking. I saw that the face under the blond hair was lined.

Suddenly Sharmila twitched. The dark-haired one had let go. The noise of the leash slithering across the bar floor was worse than the sound of the dog's claws the previous night in the Lodge. The heavy Alsatian was stalking towards her, snout lowered, ears flat on skull. I could see the teeth.

'Horst! Back, you black bastard!'

Then St James looked up and spoke directly to Romesh. Unblinking.

'It's the smell that gets them. Funny, some dogs just can't take it. Scent of a bitch in heat always gets them.'

He looked down again, the heavy key-ring now in his fist. He crashed it down on the Alsatian's rump. The brute snarled, crouched just out of range, and snapped his jaws. Sharmila's fingers dug into my forearm.

'Back!' The Alsatian crawled back towards the men, head even lower, leash still trailing.

Romesh turned to me. 'They say master becomes like dog, dog like master.' It was just as loud. 'I think therefore that my daughter is safe with homosexual dog. Drag dog. Have you ever come across before, Nigel? I would not have believed.'

I did not believe. I said nothing. And by that time my brain was reeling. Not only was it wildly out of character, Romesh wanted to involve the whole bar. All the time he had been talking like that, he had also been looking round. Especially towards the reporter who was sensibly taking an intense interest in the bottom of his whisky glass. Grass polished the same part of his counter for the third time. Fred and Ginger were looking straight ahead, expressionless.

The man in the black leather stepped forward, the dog now held back by his companion. I saw that the hair-colour was out of a bottle. His face had lost its rigidity. It was smiling, which was worse.

He ignored the rest of us.

'Your little circus tomorrow,' he said to Romesh, 'really lookin' forward to seein' it roll. I hear you've found some old tea-cups, after all your work. Insured, are they? Fragile things, tea-cups. That right, Brian?'

Behind him, the other one grunted something, too busy holding back the dog.

He hadn't finished. 'After that, you've still got to get it off this bloody island, haven't you? You and your boys. And this lovely, black-haired daughter of yours.'

He suddenly reached out as if to touch her cheek with the back of his small hand.

'Lovely skin, hasn't she, Brian?'

An inch away, St James pulled the hand back.

Sharmila fled from the bar, knocking my drinking arm hard, tears flooding down her cheeks. Romesh laid a hand on my beer-soaked fist. Then he picked up his own beer glass and drained it. He laid the glass slowly back on the counter.

'Come, Nigel, Mr Hagemann. We require to check security of stocks.'

He stepped in front of St James and made for the door. Hagemann and I followed.

As we left, the two men from the White Lodge were still sniggering at Sharmila's flight.

We were walking along the corridor. 'For Christ's sake! What were you up to in there?'

'Be quiet, Nigel. It is enjoyable being bigot. I had not realized.'

I realized. 'Not another effing caper?' I exploded. 'Next bloody time, I just hope you could let me—'

'It was not necessary for you to know, Nigel. Or Sharmila. Indeed, it is better, we thought, that you do not know.'

The 'we' hurt me most. But I wasn't going to look at Hagemann.

'You've really charged up these bastards! You realize that, do you?' I ran out of words.

'Do you think reporter took full cognizance?'

'What?' I must have goggled at both of them.

'Reporter. Was he listening fully, do you consider, to artifice?'

'Of course he was bloody listening,' I shouted back. 'Him and all the—The whole bloody bar was listening, Romesh! "Artifice"? It's *artefacts* you two should be worrying about! Whether they'll leave you with any!' I sucked in air.

'And you realize your daughter is now a quivering heap after all that verbal queer-bashing of yours?'

I rounded on Hagemann then.

'At least one of us was ready to step in there, if they'd laid a finger. Or set the hound on her.'

I kept up the stare. He said nothing.

'It is Mr Hagemann's job to show courage tomorrow, Nigel. Not tonight. These were my instructions.'

Hagemann still kept his mouth shut, staring back. I thought I could see the edges of his lips twitch.

'Is that on odd dates or even, Romesh?' I was still busy staring out Hagemann.

Still not getting a real reaction, I turned my back on him. 'We'd better double-check those locks, then.' Reaching across Romesh, I twisted and tugged at the heavy doorknob to the room with all the porcelain. The door was firmly locked.

'Mr Hagemann, you have one last task tonight.'

Hagemann nodded back at Romesh and went off. He said good night only to his employer.

'Aren't you going to check your daughter is OK?'

As we glared at one other, the big reporter came down the corridor, yawning broadly. He had to repeat his side-shuffle to get his stomach past us.

'Quite a wee ceilidh, wouldn't you say, gentlemen? You're an awful man, Mr Gopal. An awful man. But by all accounts you showed great restraint on a previous night. Not always a firebrand, then? Good night to you both.'

CHAPTER 20

Romesh opened one eye.

'How's the head?'

'Head is first-class, thank you.'

He levered himself up on to one striped elbow and opened the other eye. 'I am quite ready for Gopal Exposition.'

He sat up in the bed and turned towards me. 'You have been down to room?'

'It's OK. Amazing. Everything intact. Couldn't sleep, worrying about it.'

'Emphasis of last night to White Lodge friends of yours ensured, Nigel. I did not anticipate trouble from that quarter.'

I felt chastened. It was too early to be chastened. 'So tell me what it was you were expecting.'

'For disruption at press conference today. Little man used word "circus" in bar last night. He may attempt to make clown of me.'

He tugged upwards at his pyjama top. He had an extra spare tyre I hadn't seen before.

'That all?'

'That should be all. Cruel verbal treatment of Sharmila was necessary safety-valve which I had foreseen.'

'I forgot all that stuff last night was a blind. Pity I don't know why at the time.' He ignored that, so I pressed on.

'How was she when you went up?'

'Sharmila is most resilient young lady. She had quite recovered and was fast asleep.'

I grunted at him. 'They're villains, Romesh. It's obvious, just to hear them. All that upper-class London claptrap to impress the natives in the hotel bar before we arrived!

They're pure East End. Never been West of Piccadilly Circus—except to flog off their wares to a dodgy company of art-dealers. "St James"!' I snorted.

By that time, Romesh had gone next door and was making splashing noises. He had to shout round the corner at me, over the noise of the foaming island water.

'Reporter is too shrewd for my taste. I trust other press-men turn out to be more gullible. You must inform of moment of arrival. I shall start address at ten a.m.' He began to gargle noisily.

'Will do. After I've checked out all my leads and connec-tions.'

I left him to dress. On the bottom of his bed, laid out the previous night, was his best short-sleeved safari suit. I looked out of the high window. He was in luck; by the tiny Valtos pier, the sun was dancing a Scottish reel on the surface of the sea.

'The day is just *too* bright, Mr Carlton. That is exactly why Mr Macleod and I have decided to have a wee look-in on your friend's talk instead.' Fred nodded towards Ginger, then shook his grey head at the awful fishing weather. He took his seat in the front row, walking past the long shelves laden with porcelain without a glance. Ginger joined him, after looking at just one blue pot. He too was clearly more worried about their chances of salmon-casting that day.

I fussed with a wall-socket and tried out a playback button on the machine for the third time. Everything was ready from my side, technically.

I heard feet behind me, then the groan of an overloaded chair. The reporter had arrived too. He sat behind the two old fishermen, hat on back of tousled head. There was no sign of a pencil or pad in the big man's big hand. He smiled calmly back at me as he chatted to them about the chances of a fishing breeze that day.

Two minutes later I heard the thin jangle of the key-ring. Without any dog sounds, or a sign of his younger friend. The man they called St James picked the third row, at the back of the room, leather shoulders against the wall. No smile, of course. The little eyes seemed even smaller.

Galore and Grass came in and sat down. They started to discuss what was probably something to do with their morning schedule of work, but it was in Gaelic. Grass looked at his watch. He was already thinking ahead to his bar-opening hour.

'When do they arrive?' I asked Galore.

He crinkled his forehead at me.

'The other gentlemen of the press, I mean. The reps from all the London papers.'

He gave me that quiet, annoying Hebridean grin again. 'But all the representation you will be getting is in this room already, Mr Carlton.'

'You'll have to make that simpler for me.' I was trying not to lose my temper.

He nodded towards the reporter. 'That fellow is the *Stornoway Free Press*. At the same time he goes around the whole island of Lewis describing himself as the local "stringer"— is that the word?—for everything else. *The Times*, the *Guardian*, the *Independent*. There is not one newspaper he does not boast of representing. He is even the *Morning Star*.'

'Jesus.'

Romesh walked in, smiling at his audience.

'They're all here.'

He blinked. 'Tell,' he said quietly. Seriously.

I told him.

He sucked in air and turned towards his audience. 'Good morning, gentlemen.' He seemed to bow mainly towards the reporter. 'Welcome to Exposition of Gopal Treasure.'

I had to hand it to him. Manning the switches and buttons and taking his cue-signs in my stride, I still had time to be surprised at the confident flow. He hit every buzz-word on schedule, every phrase of sea-hunting jargon was fed in, then explained in layman's language.

He even allowed them to handle a couple of blue-glaze pieces of porcelain, watching carefully that they didn't drop a tea-bowl or a saucer.

He started with a fast description of the China Trade in the seventeenth and eighteenth centuries, emphasizing the early Dutch interest in pulling the treasures from the east back to Europe. At that stage he already sneaked in a reference to ships wandering off-course. And even bounced off his audience the thought of a Spanish galleon, split away from the Armada and lost among the Inner Hebrides. Within two more sentences, he had dropped the names of both the Dutch East India Company and the ship itself. The *De Liefde* had been driven past the Scillies, he told them, going hard north and filled with porcelain and gold.

Romesh switched time-scales then and waved his first documentary evidence. The faked read-out on continuous-stationery of a twentieth-century side-scan sonar. He even risked passing the reams of computer paper among his listeners. The reporter kept it longer than anyone else.

He said very little about the pretended oil-hunt. Instead, he jabbed at my giant blow-ups on the wall behind him—the first of the stinger, then of the bigger, fatter airlift tube, in mid-suck. My close-up of the golden Chinese shoes went down well with our audience too.

But my best shot turned out to be the one of the boys cleaning up the porcelain. The bright red gloves seemed to highlight the care they were taking. As I basked, Romesh snapped his fingers.

That was when I realized there was no Hagemann in the room. Although the hand-signal had been for Sharmila to do her walk-on, in wetsuit, somehow I thought of him. Also missing. Not there. Therefore somewhere with her, the sod.

I gave Romesh a sign back. He understood. No one else seemed to detect the brief pause before he started up again.

'We shall now move on to main part of exposition, gentlemen. We shall now see, having successfully surveyed and located sonic image out in Atlantic, thirteen miles from beautiful natural harbour of Valtos, what Gopal team was able to identify on sea-bed. Let Mr Carlton show you what magical eye of waterproofed television camera saw. Mr Carlton, please?'

I hit all the right buttons.

'Where, kindly?' he hissed.

'I could guess!'

He blinked.

'Let me go and pull on a wetsuit for you.'

'Forget, kindly. It will be out of order now that video is playing. It would be of small impact. Only your homosexual friend at rear noticed gap in exposition. I detected snigger.'

'OK.' There was something from earlier in the lecture still bothering me. 'Why the hell did you tell them Hagemann was a marine archæologist? He could be found out. That reporter only needs to look at what Hagemann does with a dig-reference grid and he'll blow the gaff on us all.'

'Do not concern, Nigel. It will become clear within one hour.'

I shut up.

'Kindly pass bag,' he whispered next. 'I must anticipate first press question.'

I lugged the locked bag over from beneath the TV monitor they were all watching so intently. It was heavy, but not that heavy. He unlocked it and pulled out the documents. This time there was no real clunk of metal against metal from inside. But as he did it up again, I saw the dull glow of a gold shoe. Something had gone from in there. I didn't know what.

We had almost got to the dangerous bit. It would be question-time after the video stopped. I sat back in my chair, listened to my own, boring voice-over, and watched the faces watching the screen.

The reporter was the calmest one. St James had lost some of the scornful twist to his bloodless lips—Romesh's expert presentation had seen to that. Fred and Ginger were engrossed. Grass looked at his watch again. And Galore was hugging himself as if he had located the treasures himself, off his own shore.

'One small question, if I may.'

Into the silence after I hit the stop button on the recorder, came the slow drawl.

'Roddy Macleod, *Stornoway Free Press* and other newspapers.' He struggled to his outsized feet.

He went straight to the weak point.

'This porcelain is very elegant and refined, Mr Gopal, but you are telling us the vessel located so professionally by you treasure-seekers is the *De Liefde*?'

Romesh's head moved sideways in agreement.

'And it is a Dutch East Indiaman straight from the very middle of the eighteenth century, you say?'

Another head-waggle.

'But how exactly, Mr Gopal, can you . . .?'

'By documentation, Mr Macleod.'

From the baize table Romesh picked up the papers he had taken out of the locked bag. He waved them at the reporter.

'These are ship's manifest documents, Mr Macleod. They agree exactly with items found on sea-bottom by Dr Hagemann. Even down to positive description of gold articles, found some metres from broken hull. We have exact match.

We have located treasure worth hundreds of thousands of pounds. At least. Do you read Dutch language?'

The big man didn't try to read them. Instead he twisted the brittle paper between his fingers. The paper crackled. He handed the faked ship's manifest back to Romesh.

He wasn't finished, though.

'But how can you link up this fine piece of paper with what you found in that St Kilda Gap of yours, Mr Gopal? I can see that it corresponds to the items on your shelves here. But how do we know that wreck out there is the *De Liefde*? Could you tell us that?'

'By end of my exposition, Mr Macleod, sir, I shall prove such connection. As we talk, my Dr Hagemann is transferring latest find from deep sea. It will give conclusive evidence both of Dutch-ness and precise identity.'

He even looked at his watch then.

'Let us hope so, Mr Gopal. It is a precise provenance you are lacking, is it not?'

'Precise provenance, Mr Macleod.' Romesh was still looking calm. The reporter sat down.

But he was not to be the only doubting listener.

'More wobbly video nasties and fast gabble? Is that what we're goin' to get next, Gopal?'

He was up on his weedy legs, hands in leather pockets. 'I've had enough of this crap!'

He began to move towards the door. 'One shitty little press conference in the Hebridean sticks won't cut ice down in the real world! Do you bloody think that this . . .?'

'Then I would bid you good morning, sir.' Romesh said it calmly.

We watched him stalk out, his tight little bottom looking properly indignant.

'Now, Mr Macleod, gentlemen, I shall beg you to excuse me also.'

And, staring down at his wrist again, Romesh left us there in the room. He actually left the bag with me.

As one man, they got up, walked over to the window, and looked out.

He was walking confidently down to the quay, the light playing on his thick hair; the bare brown forearms looking unnatural in the thin Hebridean sunlight.

Romesh was bouncing along that path like a man who had already seen a boat coming back round the headland.

As the *Girl Mairi* chugged nearer the harbour, I could make out Hagemann's irritating pipe sticking out of the wheelhouse window. I made my mind up I wasn't going to enjoy the next bit.

He came back up the steep path at a gallop, leaving even Hagemann in his wake. He was holding high the dripping, dulled metal shape by a lug in its curved top.

He came into the room in triumph, struggling to regain his breath, and marched straight for the window-bay, well to the left of his two baize-covered tables. It puzzled me why he was holding up his main exhibit against the light. I soon found out.

'Gentlemen, it is as Dr Hagemann believed. He has returned with positive proof. Ship's bell, bearing emblem VOC. Vereenigde Oost-Indische Compagnie. Dutch East India Company. And name, gentlemen. Ship's name.'

He paused and knocked a barnacle off with the side of his free hand. It came away from the metal too easily, I thought. Almost as if it had been glued on.

Romesh looked up into the tilted faces of his listeners. It is—' he peered short-sightedly—'gentlemen, it is indeed *De Liefde*. We have found precise provenance.'

WOOOOOOOOMPH!

Even with the quivering window shut and the distance that was involved, the noise was amazing. It was followed by a high, hanging plume of foam and water. Later, I worked out that the gigantic explosion had taken place a mile out to sea. To Romesh's pole-axed audience, though, it would all have happened twelve and a half miles from the shore, in his famous St Kilda Gap.

He wheeled round, mock horror shining in his eyes. He hadn't dropped the bell.

'My God!' he shouted, and turned to a wide-eyed Hagemann.

'Dr Hagemann, your hopes of undersea archæology have gone up in smoke.'

On cue, fully rehearsed, Hagemann nodded back at him. Romesh took a deep breath.

'I put this down to professional jealousy on part of person called St James,' he told the reporter.

'Terrific. One of the really great Expos.'

'Thank you, Nigel.' He was smirking, of course, his locked bag back at his left ankle.

'It was most useful to hear from you of road-blasting operations on road to Stornoway. It gave me idea.' He laughed out loud.

'I only hope Sharmila had hands in ears.' We looked at each other.

I swung round to Hagemann. 'I thought she was with you.'

He shook his head at me, still smug after his morning's work.

Romesh turned round, suddenly very serious. He was staring at the empty chair at the back of the room where St James had been sitting.

CHAPTER 21

Romesh's brain moved faster than mine.

'Ve must go up hill before hostage message comes to hotel. To reporter.'

I nodded and tried to keep up with him. We were running up the path from the back of the Loch Roag. The one thing he had done in between was to lock up the beloved locked bag in his bedroom.

I could hear Romesh's breath grow tighter as we ran. Behind me, Hagemann had almost caught up.

The weather had changed yet again. Storm clouds had pushed across the weak sun filling the whole October sky. It was becoming blacker every minute.

We stopped. Romesh was wet with sweat.

'You know house,' he wheezed, peering up towards the long, low building bathed in the eerie half-light.

'Tell vhere to break in most speedily, Nigel!' He gulped in more air.

Hagemann stood on my heel.

Thinking of the geography of the house, I told them we should go for the big room, the one controlling the central corridor.

I rummaged in my pocket. The knife was still there. I felt confident about one thing. Getting in.

The kennel, as we crept past it, was empty. Good news and yet not so good. I said nothing to them.

The catch was less stiff that time. Within two more minutes we were standing on the Persian carpet. I could feel Romesh's chest heave beside me. There was no sign of anyone. Or the things I expected to see there.

'Romesh!' I hissed. 'They've gone. The paintings. The

altarpieces. Those bastards knew we would do what we've just done. They're waiting for us!'

But at first he said nothing. Instead he grabbed my forearm with his thick fingers.

Then suddenly, 'Look, Nigel!'

He was staring into the darkest corner of the room. At the minuscule, flickering screen on the antique desk. It was a TV monitor with a two-inch screen. The picture was in black and white, but at that instant I couldn't have told you. The image was worse than I'd expected, much worse.

A tiny, monochrome Sharmila, her upper half wrapped tightly in the white mosquito netting, lay lashed down on a bed, her hands twisted behind her back. She had been stripped, her long legs spread-eagled and tied to the footrail. The bottom half of the netting had been gathered together and trailed between her thighs. It gave her minimum cover.

Romesh's fingers let go of my arm. He took a sudden step forward. Hagemann and I grabbed a shoulder each, to stop him sweeping the monitor from the desk.

As we wrestled with him, the screen image changed. The older, scrawny man was seated. I could just see the foot of the bed. Behind St James, holding back the dog, was his companion. They were both grinning into the lens. The thin voice crackled through the static of the walkie-talkie none of us had noticed. Our half of the equipment was on the black side-table, next to the desk.

'Took you a time, Mr Gopal. Findin' the White Lodge.'

He re-crossed the thin, leathered legs.

'Picture all right, Mr Gopal? Bit steadier than your pathetic effort today, I'd say.'

Between us, Romesh heaved forward, powerless.

'Tryin' to get your daughter's complexion to tone in a bit with the colour scheme, if you get my meanin'. Lighten it up. We're almost there.'

He shifted the microphone he was using to his other hand.

'Come along just as we've found somethin' a good bit more effective than gauze. More psychological. I'm talking about fear, Mr Gopal. She imagines someone's about to get on top of her. Very effective, fear, on a good-lookin' young girl. Focuses the mind. Bringin' up her colour to almost Aryan.'

Behind him, the other man sniggered. It sounded worse through the electronics.

'She's wrong, o' course. We've managed to pick out another sort of mate for her. More appropriate. Only real male in the place, Brian says.' He giggled and half-turned.

'Brian?'

Suddenly, the other man paid out half the length of the thick leash from his fist. Enough to let the dog lunge forward and plant his front paws on the foot of the bed between Sharmila's bound legs. The dog was sexually aroused.

'See what I'm gettin at, Mr Gopal?'

He sneered at the camera and moved his free hand to a control switch. The monitor blinked and returned to the first picture we had seen. Sharmila, full-length. Very slowly, the bottom half of the netting was pulled away by an unseen hand; away from her struggling legs.

Romesh wrenched his whole body free from our hands. He snatched the walkie-talkie from the low table.

'Vhat is it you are after, you bastards?' he shouted into it. 'Do you vish porcelain?'

The picture of a writhing Sharmila stayed on-screen.

'Ve vant you to give us the gold, Mr Gopal.' It was a cruel take-off.

Then the voice dropped back into its slipshod London accent.

'The gold, you ugly black bastard, then you can pack up your Chinese piss-pots and go home!'

He sniggered. 'We want the real business, Mr bloody Gopal. Drop the rubberware games with your bits of china

—they don't fool any bugger. Then get out of our territory, my untouchable friend with the touchable daughter!'

It wasn't the main bedroom.

While Romesh was suffering, I had peered at the two electronic pictures, trying to make out which room they were in. The bed filled the TV frame but I had just made out the legs of the bedside table. It was the spare bedroom. I would need to be right; there would only be the one chance.

I clicked my fingers at Hagemann. After an agonized second he understood and reached inside his blazer for the pen. I scribbled the message on a scrap of paper from the desk and pushed it silently into Romesh's palm. I didn't know whether there was another camera trained on us. He read it and acted. He started to talk continuously into the two-way radio.

I signalled to Hagemann to stay where he was. He looked relieved. Edging off the carpet, I tiptoed back towards the windows.

I ran over to the second station-wagon and groped under the taut tarpaulin. I could only force the nearside door half open. It was all I needed. I got my second idea as I quietly closed the flap to the glove compartment.

The path down to the hotel was awash. It was now almost as dark as night. In mid-afternoon. Pulling up my collar, I splashed forward, through the rain, elbowed open the door, and ran up the back stairs to my room.

I was working out the rest of my plan of action as I came down the steps again, wetsuit over one arm. Preoccupied, I closed the door behind me, turned round, and tripped over the corner of the hotel peat-stack. It saved me looking further.

Unzipping the front of the suit, I began to stuff the sodden slabs of peat inside. After ten double-handfuls, the suit was full. I bent down and hoisted the heavy, black shape in a clumsy Fireman's Lift. It had all the weight of a medium-sized man.

As I struggled up the hill against the sheeting rain, I saw that the light was on in that spare bedroom. Head down, both hands now wrapped around the midriff of my rubberized friend, I crept towards the window-sill. It was open one inch. I could hear the St James voice, live. They were both still staring towards the door.

'Right! Time you gatecrashed!' I hissed at my alter ego. I drew back my aching arms, bent my soaked legs, and hurled it at them.

The bulging wetsuit crunched through the white window-frame in a black, wet, flailing mass.

The bullet from St James's gun barely changed forward momentum of the black shape. It knocked both of them sideways and down, sprawling on the floor. The gun skittered across the bare wood.

Only the leaping dog knew the difference between me and the peat-filled shape which had hurtled first through the shattered glass. I killed the dog with the gun from the glove compartment; just before I clubbed the two men unconscious.

'Nigel? You won't ever . . .?'

'No, honey. Won't even tell them you looked ludicrous in drag.'

She smiled softly up at me from the edge of the bed and tugged at the hem of my jacket. It almost reached her knees. She began to rub a raw ankle. I went out to fetch the other two, pushing rain out of my flattened hair.

'Could easily have come out there with you, Carlton,' Hagemann told me, jaw in the air.

I turned to Romesh instead. He was staring at the TV monitor, saying nothing.

He reached across to switch off the picture of his daughter staring at the dog's body, then gripped my forearm again. This time it was a squeeze of thanks. We walked back to that smaller bedroom.

He didn't speak until we had trussed up both of them.

'Why did you choose to do this thing from outside, Nigel?' he asked.

'Saw they were all geared up for us charging through that door,' I told him.

'Besides, I knew the route. I just prayed the gun I could see in that weedy sod's hand wasn't the one he had stashed away in his spare station-wagon.'

Then I looked down at the wetsuit.

'Any ideas on how to mend a giant puncture?'

St James glowered silently back at me.

Hagemann and Romesh gave themselves the job of lugging our prisoners back to the big room and lashing them to chairs.

'Thought it was old Hagemann who'd come to the rescue first off, Nige,' she said, splaying fingers through her tousled hair. 'Then I realized it was your Mr Condom.'

She bent forward to push some spilled peat back inside the wetsuit and do up the long zipper.

He came back on his own, smiling at us both.

'It was good news. After all.'

'Oh yes?' We said it together.

'They were almost gentlemen—leaving us with porcelain. It is also good thing they did not realize gold in shoe shape is worth twenty times more than bullion value!'

He saw my eyes widen.

'Total prize is now worth one million pounds, Nigel!'

Sharmila giggled.

I spoiled it for him then. I was still bothered about something.

'Romesh, why did he leave your Expo ahead of time?' I asked. 'If his mate had already been given leave of absence?'

His face fell.

CHAPTER 22

Romesh turned round.

'How many took you prisoner?' he asked her.

'Brian, on his tod. Grabbed me in the corridor upstairs, shoved an evil rag in my face. Next thing, I was on that bed.'

'And what did older man say when he came into bed-room?'

She thought again. 'Told Brian they could now go ahead. That everything was lined up.'

Romesh stared at me.

'The boat!' I shouted at them. 'St James must have nobbled our boat! Keep us trapped on the island with the porcelain while they got away with the gold!'

We jumped up and ran out of the White Lodge, Hage-mann the last to realize and mumbling to himself as he ran.

The *Girl Mairi* was bobbing at anchor. When we arrived on the quay, Hagemann elbowed me aside and jumped on board. The rest of us watched as he ran round, testing the boat's steering and navigational gear. The inspection over, he side-stepped past the side-scan sonar and the airlift and peered briefly down into the darkness of the empty hold. Finally, he jumped lightly back on to the quay.

'Nothing to worry about,' he announced, mostly to me. 'False alarm.'

*

Sharmila saw the reporter first, through the lighted window of the hotel.

'If there's somethin' goin' on, he doesn't know about it, thank God. At his whisky bottle as usual.'

She got down from the tips of her toes.

Romesh had had to stop for breath. He leaned against the outside wall, then he blurted it out. 'Move treasure back to boat. We must act quickly. We must leave here at utmost speed!'

I started off, heading for the porcelain. Hagemann stayed where he was, feet rooted to the gravel path.

'Where are we going, sir?' His voice was tight.

'Ve shall go to Ullapool. On mainland. Then ve drive south!' He ran out of breath again.

'Why don't we just dump the survey equipment and drive the two station-wagons with the porcelain on to the Stornoway ferry?'

It was too much for Sharmila.

'Be your age, Hagemann! You're not gettin' me to trot up that hill with an armful of china just to run straight into Dr Crippen and his beloved Brian again! Ugh! Probably undoin' themselves while you're arguin' the toss down here!'

Hagemann looked sour.

Romesh made for the front door of the hotel. Over one shoulder, he said, 'On to boat. Maximum speed!'

But he wasn't going there himself. From the bottom of the staircase, he pointed a finger towards the room with the porcelain. 'I shall join you with all luggage. I shall settle up also.' He took the steps up two at a time until he reached half way.

The rest of us ran into the room and looked anxiously round the shelves.

They were full of antique Chinese export porcelain. We started to breathe normally again.

Sharmila picked up a tea-bowl and started to load up one of the bright plastic buckets with porcelain. 'Here, you two, get weavin'!' She shoved the other two buckets at us.

In twenty sweaty minutes, we had cleared the shelves and loaded the contents of the buckets back into the hold of the *Girl Mairi*.

As Hagemann struggled up the gangplank for the last time, Romesh reappeared. In his hands were two suitcases, a third and the famous locked bag were wedged under his arms. He had looped the shoulder-strap of Sharmila's large hold-all around his thick neck.

'I have gathered possessions,' he said unnecessarily. 'And paid bill.' He swallowed with the effort and straightened his arms to let his cargo drop on to the deck. My case was the one which burst open. To show everybody my wetsuit, and my dirty underwear and shirts. I kicked it shut and left it lying where it had fallen.

There were only two little lobster-boats bobbing alongside ours. They were potential pursuers. Instead of noisily smashing holes in the hulls, I tied their ropes to our stern.

'Avay!' shouted Romesh, just as I straightened up. Then he remembered a better phrase. 'Cast off!' he bawled out.

Hagemann had already started the engine. Our boat, now lower in the water with a full cargo, started to dip and weave away from the Valtos quay for the last time.

We had reached the far point of Vacsay, our friendly little island. I went back to the stern and sliced through the two tie-ropes. Sharmila joined me. We watched the two small lobster-boats, suddenly abandoned, slow and come to an indignant stop in the choppy water.

Her ears were better than mine. A quarter of an hour had passed since we had left the quayside. 'What's that slappin' noise, Nige?' she asked.

'Engine,' I guessed. 'Getting old, like me.'

'That's no clapped-out engine!' She cocked her head.

We both ran towards the hatches covering the hold and pulled them open.

'You know what that sloshin' is, Nige! It's sea-water! And it's coming from down there!' She dropped to her knees.

'Christ! Trust Hagemann!' Sharmila pulled her head back from out of the darkness and got up. 'We're awash! Water every-bloody-where down there, Nige!' She stared at me, wide-eyed.

We ran.

'Tell,' said Romesh, leaving Hagemann at the wheel. Sharmila gasped out our news.

'They meant to kill us while far out to sea,' he said simply.

It was Hagemann who had to butt in.

'Take over the wheel, sir,' he told Romesh as if nothing had happened. 'I'll pump us out in twenty seconds. It's for this sort of thing I insisted we keep our airlift operational.' He made a show of putting down his pipe.

He left the wheelhouse and strode towards the machinery.

Hagemann hit the start button masterfully and bent to pick up the business end of the thick hose. The grinding screech made him drop the giant tube.

He found the spanner which had wrecked his pumping gear jammed between the two biggest cogs. St James had been thinking ahead too.

'Now what do you suggest, Einstein?' Sharmila asked him, hands on hips. I left them to glare at each other and ran behind the wheelhouse.

Throwing the two baling buckets at them while I ran forward, I shouted, 'Bale like hell!' and jumped down into the hold in my bare feet.

Ten minutes of violent, desperate action and we knew. We were even lower in the water now, the surface of the sea lapping high and greedy at the hull; inside the hold, the long rows of porcelain were beginning to disappear beneath the rising tide of sea-water.

'We've got to get off this tub!' I told Sharmila. She threw her own bucket down, mopping sweat from her throat. We ran together towards the wheelhouse, leaving Hagemann to shout after us.

'Dad!' she said. Nothing more.

'I shall remain with ship until you are all safe,' he told his daughter and pushed his chin into the air.

'And what about the gold?' Her fast question focused his mind brilliantly.

He blinked. 'I shall require Nigel's wetsuit. Together with flippers'.

Getting what he must have thought was a poor reaction, he looked between us. At Hagemann. But his hero had gone pale. Very pale.

Hagemann was preoccupied. All at once he threw down his bright blue bucket, stripped off the blazer, and abandoned the cap. Panic written in the handsome, macho face, he pushed between Sharmila and me, past Romesh, and dived over the side of the boat.

'Chicken!' Sharmila shouted after him.

Romesh was still fiddling with the lock on the bag. Out came the fake ship's bell and the forged ship's manifest in antiquated Dutch. With a huge, stiff-arm swing, he hurled the bell over the side.

'Has served purpose!' he shouted over the noise of the splash. The bell made a fine column of white water, then sank. He had thrown it in the direction of Hagemann.

I pulled the wetsuit he had commandeered from my suitcase and dumped it at his feet. 'We're not sticking around to admire you,' I told him. I grabbed at Sharmila's hand. 'Come on, you!' I pulled her away from her father in mid-kiss.

We sprinted to the highest part of the bows through the

water sloshing around the deck. I had my shirt off and was stepping out of my trousers before she started to undo buttons. But she was the first to dive. Sharmila's underwear that day was brief and black.

I jumped after her and swallowed water. We had both aimed ourselves at the vanishing Valtos shoreline. We had a thousand yards of choppy water ahead of us.

Even from sea-level, Romesh looked less than heroic. By the time we had twisted our bodies round and trod water to look back towards the sinking boat, he had stripped off his outer clothes. Cramming the precious manifest inside the tunic section, he turned his flurried attention to the two gold shoes. At last he heard my shout and stuffed them into the heavy belt.

The boat was beginning to tilt.

He hopped forward on one flippered foot and planted the other on the top rail of the boat.

I thought of it as he was in mid-air, one arm flailing, the other gripping the gold bars. 'Romesh! The suit! It's got a bloody great bullet-hole in it!' But it was too late.

I swung round to shout at a bobbing Sharmila.

'Stay where you are! I'm going back!' I took my first, panicky stroke back towards the broad black-rubber shape as the *Girl Mairi* gave her first death-shudder behind him.

I reached my floundering boss in ten more strokes. His mouth came out of the wave and gaped open.

'Nigel! Gold shoes!' His head dipped and he swallowed more sea-water. With his free arm he was scrabbling beneath the water at the thick, leather belt.

'Sod the gold!' I bawled into his ear. 'Strip it off! Strip the thing off!' I reached out and jerked downwards at the giant front zip.

A dozen violent thrusts and turns later, he was buoyant again. The doggy-paddle was now keeping his head above most of the waves.

'Vhere?' he gasped pathetically, and spat more salt water towards me.

With one arm I wrenched his shoulders around and pointed him in the direction of the Valtos pier. I had misunderstood him again. He was still staring at me, his mouth opening and closing silently, a brown whale in a white vest.

'I've got your effing gold shoes!' I shouted, finally getting the message. 'Down my Y-fronts!'

Sharmila took over as life-saver to her father when she saw that I was beginning to tire.

We were all getting slower. Suddenly, behind us we heard the high, sighing noise, almost human. As we turned wearily in the water, the front half of the *Girl Mairi* climbed slowly upwards, quivered once, and began its long slide under the waves. Soon there was nothing to see but teasing air bubbles on the surface of the sea.

We swam on, our arms heavier with every yard.

The little island we knew so well saved us. All three of us flopped exhausted on to the white sand.

'You are having quite a day of it, Mr Gopal! One way and another!' With all the moaning and gasping from Romesh, no one had heard the soft sound of the approaching rowing-boat.

From his wooden seat, Galore was calling out over one huge shoulder. Very deliberately, he shipped the oars and stood up, his legs wide apart for balance.

'It is a good thing it was me and not that so-called reporter who took a stroll along the beach, Mr Gopal!' he said. 'Just happened to spot those wee lobster-boats on the loose. Now who could have turned them adrift, do you think?'

Romesh blinked wordlessly back at him.

The boat drifted up to us.

'There would have been compensation due to their owners if I had not rounded them up.'

Romesh saw the point.

'Compensation,' he said to Galore, and sucked in air.

'It is necessary for us to talk to you concerning loss of *Girl Mairi.*'

Galore pulled Sharmila aboard first, lifting her feet clear of the shallow surf in one easy lift. I pushed Romesh's weak-kneed bulk towards him and, with my last shove, slipped sideways—half-in, half-out of his rowing-boat. He dealt with me last.

We sat facing him in the stern of the rowing-boat, three shivering, wet schoolchildren.

'I would certainly not have enjoyed leaving you away out here to play at Desert Island Discs for ever more, Mr Gopal.'

Galore did some fancy work with one oar to turn the boat around, then dipped forward to take his first real pull at the oars.

All the time Romesh stared down at my sodden, rolled-up vest which now hid the two golden shoes. I had taken them out of my pants as soon as Sharmila had given me her first look of teasing admiration.

We caught up with Hagemann's exhausted breaststroke half way between the island and the Valtos quay.

'You can stop fetchin' help now, Captain!' Sharmila shouted down at the back of his head. 'Why don't you try the crawl? More your line!'

But she was the first to stretch out an arm to pull him out. He flopped between the seats, gasping and gaping at Romesh.

The blue eyes were still twinkling back at us as we got nearer to the Valtos quay.

'You have a spectator, Mr Gopal' Galore nodded sideways.

The reporter stood high on the concrete rampart above the quay. He had scrambled up the rusted iron hand-holds. For the first time, he had brought out his notebook. I suddenly realized that, from that height, he could see the sea beyond Vacsay. He had seen the sinking of the *Girl Mairi*.

'Never mind, Mr Gopal. It would have been worse if you had got as far out as where your wreck is. Or was. There's no island out there to be washed up on, twelve miles from the shore.'

But Romesh wasn't thinking of his own safety.

'Twelve-mile limitation,' he moaned, mostly to himself. 'Porcelain is now within twelve-mile limitation!' He was rocking sideways in his agony.

I clutched the Chinese gold.

CHAPTER 23

None of us tried to understand the words of the Gaelic song Galore was singing. We were too depressed. Crouched in the Loch Roag Land-Rover in borrowed clothes and gumboots with double socks, we stared at each other for comfort.

Our former landlord didn't feel the same. In the middle of the corner he was taking too fast, he twisted his top half around and peered at Romesh.

'I did not take you for a vindictive man, Mr Gopal. Until I saw you tear that loose shutter off an abandoned building. That was a terrible thing. Very destructive.' He chortled.

'Action was from frustration.' Romesh was still hugging himself unhappily. Then he cheered up. 'But at least we are now free of violent criminals.'

'Are you saying that the two of them have gone for good

from Valtos?' He was still looking at Romesh more than at the road ahead.

'You have seen totally empty house and absent cars?'

'I have, Mr Gopal. You may be right.' He glanced straight ahead for an instant.

'You have also seen dead dog?'

Galore pursed his lips. 'That was certainly a criminal offence in any man's book—killing his own household pet in that way. I suppose I must agree with you, Mr Gopal. It looks as if they have indeed left the White Lodge.'

To my relief, Galore turned back to look in the direction he was steering. I prefer my drivers like that. Then he flattened the pedal again, too early in the next scary bend. We were on our way to Stornoway. We skidded.

'Exactly so,' Romesh said at last. He had dropped both hands to hold on to the edge of his seat. He clamped his lips shut.

Shifting my grip on the side of smoked salmon given to us by Fred and Ginger as we left the hotel for that second time, I bent down and checked again with my free hand on the inside of my high-heeled gumboots. The gold shoes were both still there, stuffed into the top of each oiled-wool sock. They were the only valuable items we still had. They were our barter.

Beside me, Sharmila shivered in her borrowed Harris-wool sweater three sizes too big. She tugged it down over her hips for warmth. The trousers had been given to her by Ginger. They were too tight. They finished two inches above the tops of what had previously been Fred's second-best ankle-boots. She was still managing to ignore a pipe-less, bare-headed Hagemann, slumped in the front passenger seat.

Galore was now shouting over his other shoulder. 'Anyway, I am certainly glad you saw fit to come back. Not having had the chance to say goodbye to you in the proper manner, Mr Gopal!' He wheezed. 'And now, of course, we'll be seeing you one more time!' No one else said anything.

He bent his body into the next bend. 'It will give the Valtos bagpiper the opportunity to compose a pibroch in your honour.' He swung the wheel.

'What about "Romesh Gopal's Farewell to the Isles"! How is that for a title, now?' He wheezed a second time.

The first of the hairpin bends made Galore talkative again. 'Who would have thought you would have suffered two tragedies in the one day, Mr Gopal? Mind you, they were not run of the mill, so to speak. An explosion like Krakatoa itself and a sinking like the *Titanic*! I can hear Grass now, telling . . .'

He realized he'd said too much and swung himself round to peer at the darkening road ahead. We drove on in silence.

'It was a great shame, Mr Gopal—that loose-tongued barman of mine spilling the beans on your seaside activities all the time.' He looked to the front again. 'Does it help you —now that you realize his nickname has nothing to do with him dressing for ever in green?'

My boss snorted loudly. The discovery—that Grass had got his nickname because of his ability to pass on every bit of information he picked up over his bar counter—had finally ruined Romesh's late afternoon. He had learned it from the reporter, sitting by the Loch Roag Arms peat fire, wrapped in towels and with an oversized hot toddy in his hand. But none of these comforts had made him feel any better at that point.

Romesh was still scowling when Galore started on another song. It was just as impossible but less mournful.

The Land-Rover rocked round another curve. The pace slowed to 50 m.p.h. as we passed the red road-sign reading BLASTING IN PROGRESS.

Romesh winked at me. At least he was coming out of his

sulk. That day he was now as changeable as the Lewis
weather. I shut off my brain and twisted round in the hard
seat to stare out at the blur of rocks and moorland with the
scattered houses. Galore twitched us round a curve in the
road and had to swerve past three standing vehicles: two
station-wagons and a police car.

Brian was talking to the sergeant, innocent palms upwards. The chat looked as if it might be about what they
were carrying. 'Well, well,' said Galore, and pressed his foot
down for more speed.

We sped on, straining to get to Stornoway before the shops
closed. To become solvent again—and properly dressed. I
bent forward to touch the tops of the gold shoes again, just
to be sure. There would be twenty more minutes of Galore's
inspired, nerve-racking driving.

We drove into Stornoway.

'You stated gold would be marketable in this town,' Romesh
grumbled at Galore. He had had a fourth refusal from a
polite, surprised shopkeeper. Galore shut the door and
revved the engine again. 'I agreed that you had a marketable
commodity in these fancy gold blocks of yours, Mr Gopal.
I did not say who exactly would buy it.'

'Shoes,' Romesh told him.

'What do you mean by "shoes"?'

'I did not use expression at exposition?'

'You did not.'

'Each is "shoe" of gold. Chinese expression to describe
unusual shaping of antique gold blocks.'

Galore brightened. '"Shoes", is it?' He paused before he
hit the pedal. 'Now why did you not say that before, Mr
Gopal?'

We rocketed down the steep, crowded street, made a right
turn, and slammed to a halt outside a neat shoe-shop
overlooking the inner harbour.

'They tell me this is the best gold-mine in the whole of Stornoway.' He grabbed the gold shoes from an open-mouthed Romesh and ran into the shop.

'Just four thousand pounds!' Galore shouted at us as he jumped back into the driver's seat and switched on the engine. Romesh stared at the thick wad of paper in horror, turning the notes over and reading the pound signs. They were Scottish banknotes again. Galore looked down at his watch. 'There is just thirty-five minutes left for you to get all togged-up.'

He crashed the gears. 'I would have got you more money for the pair, but they were all there. All the brothers,' he explained, shaking his head. 'Most able negotiators. Told me it was not a shoe they had an everyday call for. And they would not go higher than the bullion value, Mr Gopal. What do you think of that?'

Romesh said nothing. He was still counting.

Galore slowed down as we passed one of the biggest stores. 'I told them you would be buying your new footwear elsewhere. They were quite upset to hear it.'

Romesh peeled off the top layer of the largest notes and handed them to Galore. 'Compensation for sad loss of *Girl Mairi*,' he said.

Galore thrust them into a top pocket. He pointed the Land-Rover towards the main part of town and began to weave through the traffic.

Within twenty minutes, we were newly kitted out. Sharmila even found a neat Harris Tweed outfit to show off her shape.

Galore swung us down a steep, narrow street and into a righthander. We were passing the police station. In the pound sat the two station-wagons. They were empty of occupants and empty of church art.

'I wondered,' said Galore, spinning the wheel, 'why that

reporter wanted such an official telephone number out of me at Loch Roag. I just hope he reversed the charge.'

Sharmila giggled.

It was time for pure formality. That is how Romesh had described it to us. Then all we had to do was to speed back to Valtos, properly dressed once more, to be ready for a morning of hoisting fragile porcelain for a second time.

Galore found the Customs House for him at the end of a narrow, inward-looking street leading down to the end of the thin finger of land which split the port into its inner and outer harbour.

The man in the navy-blue peaked cap was courteous and calm. Too calm. He listened to Romesh's tale, put down his unused pencil, and took a deep breath while Romesh finished his presentation.

'. . . So, purely as bureaucratic formality, since ancient Dutch vessel sank outside twelve-mile limitation, I can now officially inform you that—'

'Well now, Mr Gopal.' He scratched one ear as he broke into what Romesh was telling him, 'from what you say, even if you prove that the wreck was outside—'

'Most certainly, I—'

'Romesh!' I hissed sideways, 'It's been blown sky—'

'I can most certainly show you section of hull which—'

'Romesh! The bits are on the bottom, off Vacsay. Ten yards from—'

'Kindly do not interrupt, Nigel!' He turned back to the Customs man. 'As I was saying . . .'

'If you cannot prove to us that title has become vested in yourself, Mr Gopal, then the stuff belongs to the authorities. Whether it came from inside or outside the limit.'

The Customs man paused. Romesh's face showed me he had lost all faith in lawyers. And twelve-mile limits.

'All this valuable cargo will now come under the jurisdiction of the Receiver of Wreck.'

'And who is Receiver of Wreck, kindly?'

The Customs man tugged at the peak of his cap. 'Well now, that is me, I suppose.'

'You do not know?'

'A way of speaking, Mr Gopal. It's me right enough.' He raised his voice. 'That is so, is it not, Angus John?'

Another peak-capped head popped up from behind a partition at the back of the big room and nodded before disappearing again just as quickly. I heard a smothered snigger.

'We are therefore duty-bound to hold a public auction at the end of a year and a day from—'

'Year and day? This is feudalism! This is—!'

'You will be free, Mr Gopal, to bid at this auction although—'

'You will allow me to bid for own property! This is now racialism! I intend to report you to authorities! Your name, please?'

Romesh scrabbled at the pockets of his new suit but didn't find a pen. Instead, he grabbed the pencil in the Customs man's hand and tore a blank from the pad on the high, official counter.

'Malcolm John Macleod,' he said, calmly watching Romesh scribble.

'But that will not get you very far, Mr Gopal. The Law of the Sea applies to everybody who reports—'

'But I have not yet officially completed reporting of wreck to you, Mr Malcolm John Macleod!'

'That has already been done, Mr Gopal. We have had the porcelain reported to us already.'

'By whom?' Romesh looked around wildly.

'By the reporter, appropriately enough, Mr Gopal.' Then

he looked at me, rather than Romesh. I probably nodded back at him.

'And was there not some word, sir, about some precious metal being—?'

That was when Romesh snorted loudly, grabbed Sharmila by the elbow, and stamped out of the snug little office.

Hagemann, Galore and I trotted after them along the dark corridor towards the harbour front. The Customs man had not quite finished. He had to shout it out.

'I have to tell you, sir, that we must finally deduct our commission from the total proceeds of the public auction!'

The last sentence was even more faint. 'And charge the usual 15% for VAT on such commission!'

Outside, Romesh brushed his damp forehead with the back of his hand, sucked in crisp air, and wailed.

'Value Added Taxation! Can we never escape from monstrous British bureaucracy? It is positive end of adventure!'

Sharmila put a comforting green and tweedy arm half way round his waist. He hardly noticed.

CHAPTER 24

I don't remember much about the rest of that night. Led by Galore, we crawled round the bars. Stornoway was well supplied—there seemed to be roughly one per hundred of population. And all the shelves had an amazing selection of whiskies on offer. Perhaps he was being kind and could see he had four bombed-out people from the mainland on his hands until the ferry to Ullapool sailed.

The hotel room might well have been large and airy. All I can remember is the shape of the pillow that reared up and hit me at around 1.0 a.m.

*

The next morning, at 4.45 sharp, I was shaken awake as he had promised by an appallingly cheerful Galore. He had news.

'St James, Mr Carlton. You need have no fear. I met Constable Macleod on his night patrol. He tells me that your men and his lovely pink-chested boyfriend will not be on the morning boat with you. I gather the Island of Lewis statistics for crimes resolved have just had a major boost. In a category they had nothing in. They are very pleased.'

The march down to the quayside was chill, the sea still a flat calm in that outer harbour. A seal broke the surface just behind the high, dark hull of the ferry-boat. It snuffled loudly into its whiskers and submerged. It looked a good morning for a sail.

Romesh and Sharmila shivered beside me, Hagemann one step behind, as Galore took his farewell.

'. . . and that was a fine wee ceilidh you had us on last night, Mr Gopal!' he finished. 'You have a good singing voice on you. You should cultivate it.'

Romesh's face showed he had no recall. Galore slapped the broad, bowed shoulders. 'Never mind now, Mr Gopal. Just think! You are on your way home, away from the Highlands and Islands, going south. It will be downhill all the way for you from now on!' He probably meant well.

We all stood at the rail and waved back at the cheerful figure on the pier below. I still didn't know how much of it all he knew.

As Stornoway grew smaller, the Loch Roag Land-Rover swung round and pointed itself back towards Valtos and our lost, submerged porcelain.

'What do you mean precisely by "stolen", kindly?' Romesh rocked back on his new heels.

'It's difficult for me to be more exact than that, Mr Gopal.'

Mr McWilliam, the owner of Ullapool's biggest kippering shed, had a different Highland accent, not so strong as those on the Isle of Lewis. His brow creased, then became smooth again. 'Your van has been abducted, you could say.' He thought again. 'Purloined.'

Romesh blinked back at him.

The air in the little mainland port was bright and hard. Good listening weather. It was only the news that was bad. We had hiked up the abrupt hill from the ferry with our new suitcases. It was 9.0 a.m. Sharmila had flopped down on the top of her case and put both hands to her ears. 'God Almighty!'

'You have police?' Romesh asked McWilliam and turned round. The wide street was deserted. There was no traffic. Not even our van. Nobody was tending a garden in front of the neat rows of white-painted houses. The only sounds breaking the stillness of the long sea-loch came from the small fishing fleet below, unloading their catch at the pier.

'We have indeed. Constable Macleod. He is a Lewisman, originally.'

Romesh was unimpressed. 'And what does he say, kindly?'

'He blames the tail-end of the holiday season, Mr Gopal. We have no crime up here during the winter, you realize.'

'What compensation are you offering, please?' asked Romesh with the air of the newly-expert.

'The very moment my insurance company sends me the amount I have claimed, Mr Gopal, I shall be in touch. They are a London company, I should warn you.' He shook his white head. 'It will take some time with such a distance involved.'

Romesh seemed to shrink into his new overcoat.

*

The bus to Inverness was jam-packed. We had to scramble for the last seats. Sharmila had bought one more item after we had argued over the choice of sandwiches. She sat on the long back seat between two farmers. She was staring into space, the blue plastic of her earpieces clashing with her green tweed. One of the farmers started to whistle the same piece of pop coming from her new cassette. He was flat. It made me wish for my best jazz, now being played over on our van's hi-fi by some villain. I started to suffer serious withdrawal symptoms.

'Don't get shirty with me, woman! Just do that thing! For me. Please! Christ, I've run out of coins! See you!' I slammed down the receiver.

While I'd been making the long-distance call, Romesh had been buying the railway tickets. One-way. I had to listen to his opinion of British Rail's pricing policy. Then he remembered.

'She will be there to meet?'

'She will be there to meet.'

I picked up my case and Sharmila's. We all started to run towards the waiting train.

As the train shuffled into Euston, I unwound my cramped legs, pushed the other half of the curled sandwich between the seats, and wrestled Sharmila's suitcase from the luggage rack. Then, after all those days, I remembered my unused deerstalker.

She was standing at the ticket-barrier looking incredibly fresh. She had on a man's shirt. White collar open, with vertical candy-coloured stripes. It was one of mine.

From her high bosom, Rupert glared balefully back at me. She put the cat down, straightened up, and brushed past me.

'Mr Gopal! Good to see you!'

'Caroline. You are looking most delightful! Trouser-suiting is most flattering.'

He waffled on like that for several minutes while the rest of us cringed. But I had rehearsed him quite well. He switched smoothly to talk about his major, imaginary, property deal north of the border. He even managed to step jauntily across the marble concourse at her side as if he had had a major triumph in the Highlands and Islands.

The two girls had touched fingers.

'Don't forget you promised to send a postcard to that sweet little chambermaid of yours, Nige,' Sharmila told me as we walked, pulling her new Portuguese phrasebook from her shoulder-bag. What she'd said had been pitched just loudly enough to reach other ears.

At last Caroline slowed down, seeming to see me for the first time.

'Not all hard work then, Mr Carlton? Got in some deer-stalking, did we?' She even gave me a smile, hand to her long white throat.

I nearly said something.

We walked some more. 'Whatever became of your boss's sudden interest in religion?' She watched my eyebrow go up. 'Art. Church art. Stolen church art?'

'Ah!' I said. 'Yes. Went off it. Too religious up there. Began to put me off too.'

'Typical men,' she said.

Rupert had been picked up again as we passed through the barrier. He was suddenly paying me a lot more attention as he lay across Caroline's shoulder, looking backwards.

Then I realized. 'Oh no you don't.'

I swung the waxed paper parcel of smoked salmon away from the twitching whiskers.

We walked on. I took a deep breath of polluted London air. It tasted wonderful.

We came to my MGB. It seemed in good shape. Certainly not stolen. The bonnet was still hot.

Hagemann turned out to be a gentleman after all. And able to count seats. After the awkward silence, he volunteered to go home by taxi.

'Who was that magnificent man?' asked Caroline as she climbed in. 'Careful not to introduce me, weren't you?'

'You can have him,' I told her. 'Only one previous owner.'

I looked pointedly over towards Sharmila. Caroline didn't ask any more about him.

I suddenly remembered as I started to clamber aboard.

Struggling back from the newspaper kiosk through the commuting crowds, I found the two small paragraphs at the bottom of page six.

The Times had headlined them, INTERESTING FIND CLOSE TO HEBRIDEAN ISLAND. They dealt with the discovery of certain antique Chinese porcelain by a certain Mr Macleod. I wondered which one.

I decided that I wouldn't show the piece to Romesh that day.

Still walking, I flicked through to the Business and Finance section. The news was in its usual place. The headline read, GOLD PRICES SURGE. I wouldn't be showing that part of the newspaper to him that day either.